Also by Ellis Sharp

I0671195

Novels

The Dump
Unbelievable Things
Walthamstow Central
Intolerable Tongues
To Wetumpka
Lamees Najim

Short Fiction

The Aleppo Button
Lenin's Trousers
(with Mac Daly) *Engels on Video*
To Wanstonia
Driving My Baby Back Home
Aria Fritta
Quin Again and other stories
Dead Iraqis: Selected Short Stories

Non-Fiction

Sharply Critical

THE ORWELL GIRL

Ellis Sharp

Zoilus Press

A Zoilus Press paperback
First published in Great Britain by Zoilus Press in 2020
© Ellis Sharp 2020

The right of Ellis Sharp to be identified as the author of this
publication has been asserted by him in accordance with
the Copyright, Design and Patents Act 1988.

All rights reserved. No part of this publication may be
reproduced, stored in a retrieval system, or transmitted, in
any form or by any means, electronic, mechanical,
photocopying, recording or otherwise, without the prior
permission of the copyright owner.

A CIP catalogue record for this book is available from the
British Library.

ISBN 978-1-9997359-7-5

Jacket photograph by the Mr Triangle Agency

Cover design by The Ever-Shifting Subject

Typeset by Electrograd

ZOILUS PRESS
York, England

CONTENTS

for P

When I remember George Orwell, I see again the long, lined face that so often reminded one not of a living person, but of a character out of fiction.

George Woodcock, *The Crystal Spirit* (1967)

1 The Road to Southwold Pier

I WAS IN SOUTHWOLD, feeling lost and empty. It was October, which didn't help. The summer visitors had long since gone and the little seaside town was grey and empty. Day after day an icy wind swept in. The wind came from Russia – Siberia, the forecasters said. It arrived hurling scatterings of screaming gulls. The gulls looked black, not white. Against the colourless sky they seemed like flakes of burnt paper.

I had two people to thank for the state of things. For me being in this desolate town in a condition of mild, ebbing misery and complete isolation.

The first was Veronica. We were so good together. We met when we were in our mid-twenties. The attraction was instant. She had amazing dark eyes, jet black hair that was natural and flowed down to her waist. She was intense but outgoing. As for me: she said she liked my sense of humour. It was sardonic. It made her laugh. Plus I had blue eyes, a good figure. I was super fit. I cycled to my job in the City. I went to the gym. Plus I knew stuff, she said. She liked my angles. I read books, a lot of books. Veronica never read any, only fashion magazines.

She was part of a set and soon I was part of the set. A core of six couples, sometimes expanding to ten. All young professionals, on good salaries. Sometimes there was the soft, agreeable padding of inherited wealth.

We partied together. We went places together. There was always someone who knew someone who had a villa we could use in Tuscany. Or a house with a pool in Mexico. A marvellous place on the hills outside San Francisco. A *palazzo* on the Grand Canal in Venice. A game lodge in Kenya. There were invitations to the Maldives, to Argentina,

Barbados, Switzerland. We worked hard and played hard. It was like living in a Scott Fitzgerald novel.

But in the eight years we were together we never went to East Anglia. Veronica vetoed Suffolk. She'd heard it was flat. She'd heard it was dull.

People there went to bed at ten-thirty at the latest, she said. And not for sex. She knew that for a fact.

These golden years slid by. There were thirtieth birthday parties which in their extravagance brought to mind *The Great Gatsby*. And then thirty was behind us and we all started to feel just a little bit old. And then couples started getting married. And then the first babies arrived – super cute and incredibly time-consuming. And suddenly the set started to disintegrate. People couldn't come to Thailand because Pammy was almost full-term or because Julia – poor thing – just *had* to be with her appalling in-laws that week. Or our destination really, really wouldn't be suitable for a baby. Babies are delicate and vulnerable. They need protecting from mosquitoes and extreme heat. Plus you need to take note of prospective earthquakes, hurricanes, volcanoes, tsunamis, insurrections, terror shootings and bombs. It's hell being a white Western tourist nowadays.

Our set fell apart. It was like watching an iceberg calve and grow smaller and smaller. Soon we were down to three couples.

And then Veronica dumped me.

I had faults, I knew it. Punctuality was never my thing. I try but I always seem to end up late for meetings.

Plus I was untidy. My apartment was a clutter of stuff I hadn't put away in drawers or on shelves. The bedroom looked like the aftermath of a clothing massacre. Shirts everywhere, face down, arms in twisted positions. Towels. A score of socks which didn't seem to be all pairs. Underpants requiring the attentions of a washing machine. Stains. (Let's not dwell on the stains.)

I was quite the opposite of Veronica Fitz. Her apartment was minimalist. The only possessions that mattered were in her enormous, well-organised wardrobe. She had no books or DVDs or CDs or passé jive like that. Her apartment favoured glass surfaces, shining steel tubes, silver and black. Concealed lighting. Blinds and shutters, never curtains.

Plus, she said, I had an obsessive personality. She read an article in a magazine. She reckoned I was on the spectrum. Somewhere between madness, an autistic personality and mild eccentricity.

Maybe she was right.

When I get interested in a subject I pursue it exhaustively. I'm curious about stuff. I have phases. If it's an author, I read everything. All that they've written, all that's been written about them. I had a Shakespeare phase. I read all the plays, saw all the movie adaptations I could lay my hands on. I read two major biographies. I took V to the RSC at the Barbican, the Round House and Stratford. But she only went in the first phase of our relationship, when she was desperate to please me. Shakespeare, she finally confided, was *impossible*. All those clichés! And she couldn't understand most of it. Plus take a look at the audience! All old people with grey hair, or no hair, and groups of sullen teenagers doing their set text.

Then there was the Holocaust. I read all the major historical studies and the memoirs plus Hannah Arendt. Once, when V was away in New Zealand – it was Zoë's hen party – I took myself off to Auschwitz. I did the tour. It was winter, there was snow everywhere. Everything seemed stripped down, reduced to a terrible X-ray. The proof of a monstrous sickness.

I'll always remember the crows there. Big black birds perched on the coiled wire. And the railway track. And the terrible gate with its arched, mocking sign.

When she came back and I told Veronica she just said, 'Yech!' and then, 'I don't want to hear *a thing* about it.' History, she knew, was *horrid*.

There were other madnesses. One was my desire to see every movie Robert Mitchum ever made. (I managed around two-thirds. He made a lot of movies. There's lots I'm still half-heartedly hunting.)

Veronica said she just couldn't see the point in watching a black and white film.

Even Hitchcock she couldn't bear. *Vertigo* bored her. She closed her eyes, yawned, made her displeasure clear.

But I forgave her everything. I didn't mind. The couples I knew whose relationships lasted were always mismatched. Veronica was bubbly and fun and laughed at my jokes. Plus she was very, very good in bed. Inventive, uninhibited, greedy for pleasure. Enjoying anything, enjoying everything. That counted for an awful lot. There was nothing we couldn't resolve with a good shuddering fuck.

Eight years we were together. Eight sweet years. And then she dumped me. Just like that. No hints, no sense of an ending.

Veronica: that is the name I use to think of her now, even though she was never that.

I knew she felt guilty when she dismissed me from her service in a text message. BEN IT'S NO GOOD. I NO LONGER LOVE YOU. WE ARE FINISHED. HAVE A GOOD LIFE. She signed off as VERONICA. She was never Veronica except on her passport and airline tickets. She was always *Ronnie*.

*

I needed *something* in my life after Ronnie.

Correction. The present is as true as the past. I *need* something in my life after Ronnie.

The pain – the emptiness – lingers.

Inside an hour I'd discovered what it was all about.

Behind my back she'd hooked up with the Honourable Jonathan Gorer Firth-Habberton. He was forty-seven, newly divorced and owned estates in Scotland and Portugal. Plus a forest with a lodge in Bavaria. Plus a village in Turkey.

A village in Turkey? I mean WTF...

Firth-Habberton was a chubby chappy. He wore shirts with a green check pattern, tweed jackets and a matching cap. His cheeks were florid, his gaze avuncular. He seemed to own a lot of shotguns. He also collected vintage cars. He posed for photographs with a mansion behind him.

I guessed it wasn't his looks that had attracted Ronnie...

Being dumped was the first blow. Discovering she was serious was the second. (We'd had a couple of mild bustups over the previous eight years but nothing that had lasted.) Being frozen out by everyone in the set was the third. Nobody seemed to want to know Benjamin anymore. He was just this feller in the media that Ronnie had once had a thing with. He was toast, didn't you know? Yes, haven't you heard? She's marrying Jonny...

That was the final conclusive blow: the announcement of their engagement in the *Times*.

I was still being sucked down into darkness and whirled around by the currents of the sinking ship when my grandmother died.

*

My grandmother lived in a three-storey magnolia-coloured house in Notting Hill, with no one for company but Hilda, a live-in companion/nurse.

Granny looked like a sweet little old lady but she had a wild, wild past. I was always her favourite grandchild and she was always my favourite Elderly Relative. She wore lipstick and flirted outrageously with anything in trousers (which at her age was mainly doctors). She smoked like a chimney, had cocktails for lunch, and had a 4pm threshold after which it was okay to start in on the gin and tonics.

She liked to tell filthy stories, many of them personal. In her younger days she'd been on the fringes of the Princess Margaret set. Life was one long party. She told outrageous stories of famous men – politicians, film stars, singers. I loved her and laughed at her anecdotes and visited her often. She'd adored me ever since that moment in my childhood which I didn't remember but she did. She was always telling the story. Apparently when I was about six I'd asked her how old she was.

'Very old,' she replied. 'But a gentleman never asks a lady her age.'

Apparently I thought about this for a minute or so and then I said: 'So, granny, are you as old as Stonehenge, then?'

That slayed her.

Hilda was always fussing about my grandmother's acute cigarette habit and her drinking.

'Oh just *shut the fuck up* you silly cow,' my grandmother would gaily retort, giving me a wink.

'Now you really mustn't use bad language like that, especially not in front of your grandson.'

'I'm sure Benjamin hears worse than that every day in the office, don't you my boy?'

'Every day, granny.'

And so it would go on. They reminded me of an endlessly bickering couple in a Beckett play. Every day the same rich dialogue of complaint, reproval and reminiscence. Hilda was a spinster, fifty, briskly efficient at her nursing duties but prim, disapproving, hostile to nicotine and alcohol. She had a well-thumbed Bible in her room. I never really understood why she stayed to endure the daily blue haze of cigarette smoke and obscene tales but I think she probably felt it was her Christian duty. Plus she was amply rewarded for her labours. At the end of each day, I suspect, she kneeled and prayed for the Lord to forgive my grandmother for the mountain of sin which she laid claim to. And if the Lord has a sense of humour I feel sure that He did.

And then came the day when Hilda rang me up out of the blue one evening. 'I'm terribly sorry, Ben, but she's gone. Just like that. A stroke. The doctor's still here. Would you like to talk to him?'

And when it was all over there was the meeting with her solicitor. I discovered not only that she had left me a staggering capital sum but she'd also gifted me her holiday house in Southwold. I'd never actually been there, even though it had been vacant for years, hardly used by anyone in the family. Whenever I'd suggested a short break there Ronnie always wrinkled her nose. 'I'm not going *there*,' she'd say. 'It sounds positively *dead*. It's *Suffolk*. You know, darling, from the verb *to suffocate*. I know heaps of people who've been there and they all say it's terrifically *over-rated*.'

She always talked like that, heaping the emphasis on the end of every sentence.

And so we never went.

But now I was determined to go there. It was a house, it

was by the sea, and it was well away from London. Although I didn't think there was much chance of me running into Ronnie and her abominable beau in the capital I still didn't want to run the risk. I knew I'd never bump into Ronnie and her Honourable in Suffolk.

And I was also sick of my day-to-day routine. My life seemed hollowed-out and empty. I needed a break. Suddenly, with granny's stupefyingly generous legacy, I could afford to switch off from the rat race. I asked for a year off from my job and, because the firm didn't want to lose me, they agreed.

I sub-let my flat in Walthamstow, dumped my important personal possessions at my parents, and headed off to Liverpool Street Station.

Two trains, a taxi ride, and suddenly I was there.

Southwold.

I've read about it in the newspaper travel supplements. It's always popping up in the 'Ten Best Seaside Resorts' lists.

Family-friendly. It attracts the London media set (I smile, queasily). They call it Notting Hill on Sea.

In summer it's all sandcastles and beach huts and a pier in the distance. But now it's winter and the town seems empty and grey. When I step out of the taxi I feel the sharp bite of a northerly wind.

It's not yet noon.

Shivering, I set off to find my new home.

I have a bunch of three keys and a solicitor's letter with the address: *Vancouver Cottage, North Cliff.* That's all.

I meet a postman towing his cart and ask directions. He frowns, thinks, then remembers. He points me towards where the land drops away and there is only sky. He waves his hand again: 'Take the path. You'll see it.'

He has a Suffolk accent: deep and dragging and richly rural.

My grandmother's house overlooks the ocean. It's one of a string of quirky seafront properties built beside the clifftop path between Gun Hill and the triangle of lawn below the lighthouse. Gun Hill is a grassy dome topped with a row of ancient cannons, beyond which lie sand dunes and the distant harbour. The lighthouse is inland, marooned among cottages and Edwardian villas, set well back from the crumbling lip of the steeply sloping grass-covered incline.

At the foot of the cliff is an endless line of multi-coloured beach huts, a narrow promenade, a strip of sand and the big restless, rolling sea.

Every house is different to its neighbours. They've been built at different periods. Some are fisherman's cottages, others much grander establishments, built of Portland stone, half-way between neo-classical and art deco.

My grandmother's house is the third sort. There's a sign on the gate. 'Vancouver Cottage' was the name when granny bought it. Nobody knows why it's called that.

There are blinds down over every window. The front garden is a narrow strip of big bluish beach pebbles. Weeds are everywhere.

The place looks like it's been empty for a long time.

The architect liked towers, so from the second floor protrudes an eccentric extension somewhere between a pillar box and a greenhouse. It has a small balcony with white wooden railings. The house is painted pink, with yellow stripes. It looks like a child's birthday cake.

I try the Yale keys until I find the one which fits. I push the door open against a heap of junk mail and leaflets.

It opens directly into the living room at the front. The house smells damp and cold. I pull the blind up and let daylight pour into the room.

Inside, the cottage is smaller and darker than it looks from the path. The furnishings are cosy but spare. Beyond the living room is a small kitchen and larder. The larder has a door in the wall. I unlock it and find that it leads down by a flight of very steep and narrow stairs to a small cellar lit by a single bare bulb. Under its weak glimmer I make out a big dark rack of wine bottles, stacked floor to ceiling.

Upstairs there are two bedrooms. The smallest one, at the rear, is empty apart from a table and a chair. The other one has a double bed, a mahogany wardrobe and a spectacular view. Under a sky the colour of a bruise there are ships on the horizon. They look flat and low and long, like tankers.

What looks like the door to a built-in wardrobe turns out to be a dark, steep, narrow flight of stairs illuminated by a single bare bulb. At the top there's another door. It opens to a tiny room, icy cold and filled with light. This is the tower room, barely big enough to hold the sun-faded armchair which is its only item of furniture. A flimsy partition door opens to the balcony. The wind rips through the railings and beats against my ribs.

This would be a terrific place to sit on a warm summer's day.

I return downstairs.

The third key unlocks the back door.

There's a walled patio garden, with a circular metal outdoor table and two metal chairs. A rose with blotchy leaves is clinging to life against the high flint wall which separates the property from next door's garden. Moss has settled in between the cobbles. A single forlorn terracotta pot contains nothing but weeds.

Back in the kitchen I see a pile of instructions which granny left for visitors.

There's one for the heating. I turn it on and the boiler roars into life.

Later the pipes all over the cottage start throbbing and sputtering. It's like warmth and movement returning to the veins of something long dead.

I unpack in the main bedroom and settle in.

This place suits me fine.

I go out that afternoon to the town's only electrical shop and buy myself a CD player with speakers. There's a store on Queen Street which sells CDs. I buy a mixture: jazz, classical, rock. Retro background music for my lonely winter.

I feel fine. I've pretty much stopped thinking about Ronnie. I'm taking a long vacation from the acrid state of things. I'm more or less fine, apart from an ache deep inside me.

I look at myself in the mirror. I've lost weight in recent months and my thin, long face looks even thinner and paler. There are two lines across my brow which weren't there a year ago, I could swear it.

I'd grown a hipster beard when they became fashionable but when Ronnie cut me loose I shaved it off. I needed to change my identity in some way, no matter how superficial.

To compensate I've let my curly black hair grow a little longer and thicker.

Benjamin Alex George Turner, I say to myself: *You will survive.*

It's not yet ten-thirty and I've gone to bed. The streets of Southwold are sunk in darkness and silence.

I suddenly realise there's a regular London sound I'm not hearing.

Sirens.

There are no wailing sirens slicing through the night. Just one low inescapable pulsing and strangely soothing sound. Womb noise. More music than noise, though no one composed it.

The sea, the sea.

I lie in bed, hearing the low continuing roar and swish of the waves crashing on the beach. The ocean's heartbeat.

I listen to it, letting it wash me away into the realms of sleep.

I know what it is I need to blow away the wintertime blues. I feel a hunger. I need *something*.

Some kind of adventure or engagement.

Some new obsession.

And then, quite unexpectedly, I find it.

2   Scarlet Woman

NEXT DAY.

I explore the town. A quick first investigation.

The wind finds its way past my scarf and under my coat. The sea is a turbulent, raked mass of white horses. The waves crashing on the shore are reaching the promenade. They explode, splattering the beach huts. It's a much colder day than it looks from that grey-blue sky and the strip of lurid sunlight beyond the pier.

I head out along the cliff top path as far as the building at the end of East Street. Here, two topless women look past me, flaunting their pale, perfect bodies. Their nipples are engorged, as if both are in a state of excited sexual anticipation.

The one on the left has her arm wedged between her breasts and is pointing upwards. Her companion has an arm stretched out as if about to pat the head of a small child. Their gaze is focused on the sea.

Mermaids. These distinctly erotic stone figures were put here to lure seamen into the Sailors' Reading Room. Apparently it was built by a Victorian philanthropist who wanted to discourage them from heading for The Lord Nelson next door. The idea was that the exhausted mariners could avoid the demon alcohol by popping into the Reading Room and relaxing with a newspaper and a nice cup of tea.

Good luck with that.

I shiver and turn off, heading for the town centre. The flagpole rising from The Swan shakes and rattles. I turn off down Church Street. I walk to the end, then turn off to East Green and back towards the church. I'm holding a tourist information map which I found in a drawer at Vancouver Cottage. This is an exploratory wander around the town, to get the feel of the place.

The only other person out this morning seems to be an old man standing by a car with an open boot. He's parked beside a bottle bank. He lifts out a black lidless plastic box. The necks of wine bottles protrude from the box. The old man reaches down and begins stuffing them one by one into the small hairy mouth of the container. Engrossed in his task he doesn't notice me pad past. I hear the muffled crash of breaking glass.

I walk by a small, triangular green and enter the churchyard. Drifts of brown leaves dance among the gravestones.

Beyond the churchyard there's a children's playground. No kids – just an elderly couple sitting on a bench.

I follow the path that cuts across it and come to another small triangular green. This one is framed by a privet hedge and planted with shrubs. My town guide informs me these greens were built as fire-breaks, after half the town burned down in a great fire in the seventeenth century.

I meet the road that enters the town from the west. In fact there's only one road in and out of Southwold. It's effectively an island, with the sea on one side and marshland on all the others.

I pass a small row of shops and a hotel with a mock-Tudor frontage and leave the town behind. I soon come to Might's Bridge, which has a sign saying it was opened in 1926.

I stare down from the white railings. The bridge crosses a narrow channel of stagnant, weed-choked water. Apparently this was once a navigable waterway. There are footpath signs which point to walks along the banks but I'm still wearing my town shoes and the paths are churned to mud. Another day.

I walk back into town.

I am half-way down the main drag and suddenly the town has come alive. Cars manoeuvre into parking bays. People come in and out of shops. It's gone eleven.

Up ahead of me, on the other side of the road, a woman is standing by the kerb, focusing a camera with a stubby lens. She's taking photographs of a building on my side. She stands out because she's young, she's taking photographs and she has amazingly bright red hair.

In Southwold most hair is grey or silver. In the short time I've been here I think maybe I've never seen so many old people before, concentrated in a single place. Leastways not since I used to visit my Aunt Jane in a nursing home in Wiltshire.

I walk on, towards whatever it is she's so keen on capturing on film. Her finger presses down on the shutter button at least a dozen times. A serious photographer: most people would just use their phones.

As I get closer I'm about to stop so that I don't get in the way of whatever it is she's taking pictures of. But she stops and slips the camera back into its case. She looks to be about thirty. Slim figure, tight blue jeans, puffa jacket. And that lurid hair. The word 'red' doesn't do it justice. It's poppy-bright. In-your-face scarlet. The colour of a woman who is not afraid to be noticed; who is confident in herself. It must be coloured. Surely that's not a natural shade...

She wears it very short, like a helmet. Shorter. Like a boy's. Cropped hair. An Eton Crop, that's what it used to be called. I remember Ronnie's fashion magazines: that's where I've seen the style.

The red-head glances at me, then turns and walks away down a side street, in the direction of the Common.

A moment later she's gone.

21

I reach the building she was so interested in.

It doesn't look particularly fascinating. A double-fronted house which is joined on to a vet's practice on the far side. It's vaguely reminiscent of a house in a Jane Austen movie, so maybe it's Georgian.

The house is built of red brick. There are five windows and three of them have blinds drawn down. It has an unoccupied look.

The house has a blue front door and a shallow porch framed by pillars which are classical in their design. They might be genuine heritage Georgian architecture or they might be retro-fitted plastic. I rap my knuckle gently against a pillar.

It's stone, without question.

The door is very slightly lopsided, as if warped by either damp or heat. A Georgian house, then.

I notice two circular plates which have been fixed to the brickwork to combat structural movement. Always a bad sign in a house. A house surveyor would really go to town on those.

They have studs in the middle of the plates.

Makes me think of the mermaids...

Some of the window frames have been messed around with. The ones to the left of the front door don't match the ones to the right. It's the ones on the right that look like they're the original ones.

The house has a name. I didn't notice it at first. Its way above the heads of passers-by, between the first-floor windows, embossed on a strip of yellow sandstone: *Montague House.*

Whoever Montague was...

And below it there's a little stone tablet.

Again it's way beyond eye-level, slightly higher than the roof of the porch. Easily missed. I'm sure I wouldn't have spotted it if the red-haired woman hadn't been taking pictures.

I struggle to make out the words. The tablet is in a poor condition, the stonework is crumbling away and it's hard to decipher some of the letters.

THE AUTHOR
GEORGE ORWELL
(ERIC BLAIR)
1903-1950
RESIDED IN THIS HOUSE

So that's it. Mystery over.

The red-haired woman is an Orwell fan.

I walk on down the High Street.

I had no idea George Orwell once lived in Suffolk.

I try to remember everything I know about him.

He was a policeman in Burma. Then he gave it up and began dressing as a tramp and getting into socialist politics. He wrote a book about working-class life in Wigan. Then he fought in the Spanish civil war and wrote a book about that. I can't remember the title, something about Catalonia? Then he worked for the BBC and after that he went to live on a remote island off the Scottish coast and wrote *Nineteen Eighty-Four*. But he suffered from tuberculosis and died soon after finishing the novel. Just before he died he married a young woman called Sonia.

Something like that...

I've only read two of his books. As a teenager I read *Animal Farm*. It was okay but a bit weird. I've never felt like going back to it. It was a satire on the Soviet Union but all that was long ago. There was a pig who was supposed to be Stalin and a young boar that was Trotsky. But then Communism collapsed and faded, along with satires on it.

And I read *Nineteen Eighty-Four*, some years ago.

I remember finding parts of it quite heavy. I think the book quotes extracts from an imaginary book about politics. I skipped those pages. But I remember the end. That cage which is fitted over your face, with just a wire gate separating you from two starving rats. Who could ever forget that image?

Plus I saw the movie, the one with John Hurt. I remember it as dark and miserable. Grim. Hurt was wonderful, though. Ravaged and broken. Like he was living up to his surname.

I walk on, passing a post office and a bank. After this there's a bookshop and on impulse I go in.

It's like they've been expecting me.

There, just inside the door, is a shelf full of Orwell stuff. Some of the books he wrote, plus a biography.

I decide to start with the biography, a paperback edition of Orwell's letters and his first book, *Down and Out in Paris and London*. I buy them and then walk on until I come to a coffee shop. I go down some steps into a basement.

I order a cappuccino.

I start looking at the biography.

The next two days it rains.

I stay indoors, drinking coffee and reading. The soundtrack to my life is jazz and some Erik Satie piano pieces. Music that's gentle and not too distracting.

The rain crackles against the windows.

I dip into *Down and Out in Paris and London*. It's a fragmentary book, full of small stories.

The biography is by D. J. Taylor. It's fluent and very readable. The Southwold section is fairly early on in the Orwell saga. After prep school and Eton but before Burma, Wigan and Barcelona.

I learn that Orwell came to Southwold after his final term at Eton. He was eighteen years old. He only came to Southwold because his parents had just retired to the town. Back then it had a substantial Anglo-Indian population, so it was full of people like themselves – expatriates, who'd served the British Empire in India and had now returned to England. Orwell's father spent his whole working life in India, servicing the opium industry, back in the days when – *historic irony* – the biggest drug dealer in the world was the British government.

Orwell's mother was twenty years younger and half-French.

The Blairs had three children. Orwell, like his older sister Marjorie, was born in India but spent his childhood and adolescence in England. During these years he saw very little of his father, who he remembered as a gruff old man, forever saying: *Don't*.

There was a younger sister, Avril. She was in Southwold too. Orwell's parents lived at a number of properties in the town before buying Montague House, their final home. Their first house was 40 Stradbroke Road, on the same street as the lighthouse. Orwell lived there for less than a year. He arrived in December 1921 and started attending a small private school nearby which crammed pupils for imperial exams, including the one Orwell was intending to sit in June, for the Indian Police Force. He passed and in October 1922 set sail for Burma.

He came back to Southwold on leave five years later, having decided to chuck in his job as a cop and become a writer. His father went ballistic, so Orwell left Southwold. He rented a room in London and started dressing as a tramp and staying overnight at doss houses. Next he spent two years in Paris, hanging out with low-life types. He got a job as a dishwasher at a posh hotel. Then he returned to Southwold to live with his parents and write up the saga of his adventures.

Publishers turned it down. At Faber, T. S. Eliot said the manuscript was scrappy and unpublishable. But Victor Gollancz accepted it. This was the moment when Eric Arthur Blair decided to change his name to George Orwell. 'George' after the King and 'Orwell' after the Suffolk river.

After various alternatives were rejected the book was finally published on January 9, 1933 under the title *Down and Out in Paris and London*. It received rave reviews and made – *respect* – the *Sunday Express* bestsellers list.

It sold out and there was a second print run. Orwell had arrived. After five years of trying to become a proper writer he finally had a book published.

Orwell received an advance of £40 for his first book – not nearly enough to live off. So he found a teaching job but then he fell ill and came back to spend almost a year at Montague House. He wrote *A Clergyman's Daughter* in this house. A lot of *Burmese Days* was written in Southwold. Next he sketched out *Keep The Aspidistra Flying*.

So. There's a lot of literary history in that house with the faded memorial plaque.

Plus he fell in love with two local women.

He was besotted with Brenda Salkeld, who was the gym mistress at St Felix School for Girls. But she only wanted him as a friend, not a lover.

He had better luck with Eleanor Jaques. She was four years younger than Orwell – a vivacious, black-haired beauty. The only snag was she was the girlfriend of Orwell's best friend Dennis Collings, who was the son of the local doctor. That relationship didn't work out.

Orwell tried others.

This is where D. J. Taylor has a scoop. He explains that back in the 1980s he was at college with a girl named Annie Summers. Her father had had a very personal encounter with George Orwell in Southwold in 1934. Orwell had been loitering at Southwold harbour, waiting to meet Mr Summers's then fiancée, Dorothy Rogers. Someone tipped off Summers that his girl was being chatted-up behind his back. There was a confrontation and a chase over Southwold common. It ended with the enraged Summers pushing Orwell over the edge of a steep bank: 'I sort of pushed him off... I didn't kill him.'

A steep bank on Southwold common – I need to find out where this is. *I want to see where George Orwell was tipped over the edge.*

A couple of years after the brawl on Southwold common, Orwell, back in London, met Eileen O'Shaughnessy. They were married in Wallington, Hertfordshire.

He brought his new bride on a visit to Montague House.

She said Orwell's father was the nicest member of the family. But others remembered Mr Blair as snobbish and short-tempered, with an inflated sense of his own importance. Sometimes he'd 'try it on' with the ladies of the town. But evidently he was on his best behaviour with his sparky new daughter-in-law.

A third day of rain.

I'm reading George Orwell, *A Life in Letters*.

Orwell was a prolific letter writer.

What interests me are the letters to Brenda Salkeld and Eleanor Jaques. Both women seem somehow *elusive*. Taylor's biography doesn't include a photograph of Brenda and I want to know what she looks like.

There's a letter to Brenda. Orwell wrote it in the summer of 1934. She was on holiday in Ireland and he was in Southwold. He tells her how he nearly died of cold. He walked out to Easton Broad and the water looked so tempting he stripped off and went skinny-dipping. Then all these people suddenly turned up and sat watching. 'Among them was a coastguard who could have had me up for bathing naked, so I had to swim up & down for the best part of half an hour pretending to like it.'

He adds: 'Do come back soon, dearest one.'

Where is Easton Broad? And what is it exactly – like a Norfolk Broad?

The editor of the letters doesn't say.

D. J. Taylor cites the letter but he doesn't say anything about Easton Broad either.

Hell, *I want to know*. I *need* to know.

It's my obsessive nature coming out...

I want to see the place where George Orwell went skinny-dipping.

I brought my laptop with me but I promised myself to avoid the net and keep my phone switched off. I'm here to chill, not to get agitated. Information is an addiction like any other. But already my resolve is crumbling. I need to do some research.

I discover Orwell wasn't the first figure in English literature to go to Easton Broad. Edward Lear was staying in Southwold. He went for a walk and came across it. He was thrilled by the solitude. Easton Broad seemed like somewhere out of time. He wrote it was 'So remote and quaint and East Anglian that one feels it were in the time of Edward the Confessor.'

Lear wrote a poem while he was staying in Southwold, 'The Daddy-Long-Legs and the Fly'. The critics reckon it's a heartfelt homo-erotic love poem disguised as whimsical fantasy.

Easton Broad had a similar impact on Algernon Swinburne, a Victorian poet who nobody reads anymore.

In 1875 he stumbled upon it while making a visit.

I have found a place that would have delighted Shelley – a lake of fresh water only parted from the sea by a steep and thick pebble-ridge through which a broad channel has been cut in the middle a little above the lake, to let off the water in flood-time; half encircled to the north and west by an old wood of oaks and ash-trees, with a wide common beyond it sweeping sideways to the sea.

Cool.

I walk out through the pouring rain to the bookshop. I buy an Ordnance Survey map of Southwold and the surrounding area.

Back at Vancouver Cottage I scrutinise the map and soon find Easton Broad. It's about a mile north of Southwold.

The map shows it as a small lake separated from the sea by only a tiny strip of beach.

Next morning the light glows hard behind the curtains. Sunshine. The sea is a glittering sheet of gold. There's not a cloud in the sky. It's like a summer's day. Hot. Strangely hot for the time of year. I set out into town but quickly take off my scarf and tuck it in my bag.

I pass the mermaids but look away.

The sexual impulse, not to put it any higher, is a fundamental impulse, and starvation of it can be almost as demoralizing as a physical hunger.

You said it, Georgy boy...

(In *Down and Out in Paris and London*: that's where.)

I'm heading for Stradbroke Road. It's just a few hundred yards away. Southwold is small and compact. In this town nothing is ever very far away. I find my way to the white lighthouse and go past it. I'm looking for number 40. It's half-way down the street. An end of terrace house in a row of Edwardian properties of the kind which might be found in any outer London suburb. Front door, living room window, upstairs bedrooms, a window in a room protruding from the roof. Above the porch is a name: BRIGHTMER VILLA. A slightly pretentious name, really. This is a narrow terraced house, not a large, detached villa.

And Eleanor Jaques was the girl next door. But *which* next door? Number 38, which has a large front garden and is set well back from the road and marks the end of a separate terrace of houses built in a different style and at a different time? Or number 42, which shares a party wall with number 40? I decide Eleanor must have lived at number 42. But I don't like uncertainty. I need to check this out.

I walk on to the end of Stradbroke Road and take the road to Southwold Pier.

Back to the seafront.

I'm on the long wide path which follows the line of the cliff, gently descending to the pier. Southwold Pier is a long, low black silhouette against the bright ocean and the low, dazzling morning sun. The box-shaped two-storey building at the pier entrance looks like classically Thirties architecture. Was it here when Orwell was in Southwold? That's another thing I need to find out.

It's very quiet. A solitary fisherman stands by his rod at the pier's end.

The dangling letters which spell out the words SOUTHWOLD PIER above the entrance gate tinkle softly like wind-chimes.

I walk past. Not today. I'll check out the pier some other time. Today I'm on my way to another place.

I walk through a big empty car park on the far side of the pier entrance. Beach huts are stored at the back, safe from the winter storms which lash the promenade. Beyond the car park is the summer overflow car park. I walk across rough gravel to the sea defence wall, which curls up like a concrete wave. There's a path along the top with a metal fence. It leads to a concrete stairwell which goes down to the under-lip of the sea wall. Here a sequence of wide steps drops down to the beach and its lines of rock groynes. I walk north, away from Southwold, to where the sea defences end. Here, beyond the final groyne, a low earth cliff tumbles to the beach, its base propped up by a chaotic heap of concrete blocks.

I scramble down the rocks to the sandy beach. Someone has been here before me. A trail of footprints from some other solitary walker leads away into the distance. Small feet, by the look of it.

The beach is empty, however. It stretches away to the north, a long gleaming belt of pale yellow sand below a line of cliffs.

Beyond the heaped blocks the beach opens out into a small bay, where the tides have taken a bite out of the land.

I walk on, keeping close to the sea's edge. The waves fall gently on the beach. Everything feels tranquil and at peace.

I'm struck by how golden these cliffs are, under the blazing sun. They really do look like gold. The cliff is topped by a thin layer of soil little more than a foot in depth. Intermittent patches of green vegetation show along the crest. A knob of wiry bush. A few strands of thistle.

I walk on, noticing all the signs of coastal erosion. The dark outline of a car-sized stone structure protrudes from the surface just a few yards offshore. Some old wartime building, presumably. It looks black, coated in barnacles and weed.

The sandy cliffs aren't holding out too well against the tides. All along the base is a secondary layer of fallen matter where the undermined cliff has sheered off and dropped. Sometimes whole chunks of cliff have slipped down, bearing slices of grass from the field above.

I walk on.

A pair of pink houses comes into view, perched perilously close to the edge of the cliff. They don't look as if they have long before the sea reaches them. From the cliff below them a long blue stretch of blue plastic piping dangles, like a severed nerve. Just below the crest of the cliff there's a snapped-off brown pipe looking like the last nicotine-stained tooth in an old man's mouth. Exposed breeze-blocks in the cliff face signify traces of some older, vanished structure.

A tree in leaf lies at the bed of the cliff, still clinging onto life after being severed from the land above. Its roots are exposed. They billow out slim and wavy like the floating tentacles of a squid.

I walk on.

The cliff dips down to beach level. Here the farmland beyond has suffered from incursions of the sea. A huge horseshoe-shaped tract of once green field is soured and deadened by some past surge of salt water. Beyond where the sea has overflowed onto the land no crops grow. The farmer has given up all hopes of cultivation in this inhospitable environment.

And now the cliff rises up again, a slowly curving bend of geological beds squeezed and moulded in an era when the planet was young. This section of cliff consists of golden sandstone on a narrow bed of dark clay. Above the clay lies a seam of large white shells. This seems to be the bed of an ancient beach, when the sea level was higher than it is today.

I find a stick on the beach and dig some of the shells out. They are shallow and curved and the size of the palm of my hand. But when I touch one it cracks open and crumbles to dust. I did not know that fossils could possess such fragility.

I walk on.

Soon the cliffs curve back down to beach level.

A yellow sign on a pole embedded in the sand warns of deep water and indicates a bridge.

Ahead, a stream cuts across the beach and runs into the sea. It doesn't look particularly deep but it's far too wide to jump over. I could take off my shoes and socks and wade across but the bridge seems the simpler option.

The bridge crosses the stream, framed on both sides by thick swirls of sand. The bridge itself is buried under soft, powdery sand. I follow the trail of small footprints across to the other side.

There's a big cluster of seagulls standing on the beach fifty yards away. They register my presence and one or two take flight, unnerved by the intrusion. A few more follow, then suddenly the others rise up as one. They form a big screeching, animated cloud which moves out to sea. Then they drop down and settle on the surface.

I walk a few more yards and see it for the first time.

Beyond the bridge is a lake, separated from the ocean by a wide bank of shingle.

This is the place I was looking for: Easton Broad.

On three sides it's surrounded by reeds, bull rushes and tall, waving grass. It's a magical place.

There's not a soul around.

Do I dare to do what I came here to do?

Yes.

I strip my clothes off. I don't feel at all cold. There are a few streaky clouds but it still feels very hot.

I wade in. The water feels like ice but that's to be expected.

I throw myself forwards and begin swimming to the far end.

It's 1934. I'm George Orwell, skinny-dipping in this lonely lagoon.

Woo-hoo!

But unlike Orwell no one comes wandering over the ridge to sit on the bank and watch. There's no official who might arrest me for indecency. And when my swim is over I'll have no Brenda to write to and tell of my adventure...

The water starts to feel quite warm after the first two or three minutes. I swim to the far end and round the bend, disturbing a family of coots, who paddle frantically away and vanish into the reeds. Then I turn and swim back to where I started from.

I brought a towel with me, just in case my actions matched my ambition. I return to my pile of clothes and my rucksack and begin briskly towelling my shivering flesh. And that's when I sense it.

Someone is watching.

I don't know why I know this but I do. I continue drying myself – back, buttocks, crotch, shins. I casually turn, to see if I can spot someone.

The bank of shingle is empty and so are the dunes back where the bridge is. The reeds look impenetrable.

Odd.

I could have sworn I felt it. Some ancient primeval knowledge of when you know you're being watched. Something written into the DNA of *homo sapiens* from the era of caves and mammoths.

I must be mistaken.

But when I get to the bridge I see a third set of footprints. The small feet, and then my own, with a distinctive ribbed pattern from my boot's tread. And then the small feet, returning.

When I'm over the bridge I can see the person. They're a long way up the beach, heading back into Southwold. I don't have binoculars with me so I can't see who it is.

It's just a person, a black shape of indeterminate gender. They're almost at the first line of groynes, where the sea wall begins.

The figure vanishes, lost in the dark colours of black rock and shadowy cliff.

Twenty minutes later I've reached the same place. I've jogged along the beach, hurrying to beat the tide. I'm not seriously concerned – I could always take off my shoes and socks and wade the last bit, or scramble over the jumble of concrete blocks which litter the base of the final cliff.

No worries. Though the tide is rushing in there's still a good yard of exposed sand to get to the groyne. I scramble up to the steps below the sea wall and return to the concrete stairwell leading up to the top of the sea defences.

Instead of heading off back across the car park I make for the promenade north of the pier. It's strewn with pebbles thrown up by waves crashing against the base. But today the sea remains calm. The sun continues to burn down. It's a hot day and some day trippers have started to arrive. The car park is filling up and there are people walking on the pier.

As I get closer to the pier I notice there's someone at the place where the fisherman was earlier. But this person doesn't have a rod. They're standing on the T-shaped platform at the very end of the pier, where ships sometimes still dock to take on passengers.

It's hard to make out much about this individual. Only one thing stands out. That's the shock of bright red hair.

It's her, it must be. The one who was photographing Montague House. The one who triggered my interest in Easton Broad.

The Orwell girl.

I hurry to the end of the promenade, climb over the waist-high winter floodgate and its protective layer of sandbags, and head for the pier entrance. This is on the south side, beyond the entrance to an amusement arcade and a kiosk selling candy and souvenirs. It takes forever to get to the entrance. There's a family blocking the way, chattering, then an old man on a mobility scooter the size of a Mini and then finally a woman with a dog on a half-mile-long lead, who takes ages to reel in her precious Rufus.

At last I manage to get past and on to the pier.

I walk briskly past the restaurant, the games room, the coffee bar and a store displaying lanterns, scarves and mugs. Beyond the store the pier opens out to the T-shaped platform.

I'm acting on impulse. I'm not really sure what I'm going to say to the Orwell girl. Something along the lines of *thanks-for-making-me-interested-in-George-Orwell.*

Or maybe, *Hey! I just went swimming where Orwell did!*
Or maybe none of those things.

And anyway, she may not be all that interested in him. She just happened to be passing Montague House and spotted the plaque and decided to take a couple of pictures...

My feverish thoughts don't matter anyway.

The end of the pier is empty.

She's not there.

She must have walked down the other side of the pier while I was hurrying to the end. I go round the end of the shop and lock but I can't see her.

Maybe she's gone into the shop.

I go and check.

Not there.

I look towards the end of the pier but I can't see her. That red hair is very distinctive. She'd be impossible to miss.

I return to the pier entrance along the path on the north side. There's a line of full-length crazy mirrors set in the wall. I watch myself morph into strange shapes as I pass by. I become eight feet tall, with stick legs and a head the shape of a folded umbrella. Then I'm flattened by gravity and transformed into a grotesquely small, swollen, toad-like creature. Then normality returns – apart from the way my ribs float away from my torso in dark shimmering blobs. Then I'm past the mirrors and turn off by the end of the restaurant to rejoin the main walkway. And as I return to the pier entrance I see what I missed the first time round.

I was in such a hurry I didn't even notice it, painted on the side wall of the pier snack bar. A huge, familiar face.

George Orwell.

Big George is watching you.

It's a stunning mural.

In your face: Orwell's face. Impossible to miss. Unless, of course, you are rushing past in pursuit of a mystery red-head...

The mural is surrounded by famous Orwell quotations.

He who controls the past controls the future. He who controls the present controls the past.

All animals are equal but some are more equal than others.

Good writing is like a windowpane.

It was a bright cold day in April, and the clocks were striking thirteen.

I notice that the mural is protected on either side and from above by CCTV cameras. How very – what's the word? – *Orwellian*.

I leave the pier and walk back to Vancouver Cottage.

3   Gentleman's Relish

I NEED TO RE-READ Orwell's books. Mercifully, he wrote only six novels and three full-length non-fiction books. All the other stuff is essays, books reviews, letters, poems, plus sundry scraps and leftovers.

I was planning to avoid the internet but that's impossible if you want to acquire second-hand books.

I've started sending off for a stash of Orwell material. Firstly, all the biographies. Apart from D. J. Taylor's the only one that's still in print is Gordon Bowker's *George Orwell* (2003). But before them came Peter Stansky and William Abrahams with *The Unknown Orwell* (1972) and *Orwell: The Transformation* (1979). They were followed by Bernard Crick, author of the first 'official' biography, *George Orwell: A Life*. Then, in 1991, came Michael Shelden's account, provocatively titled *Orwell: The Authorised Biography*. A decade later came *Orwell: Wintry Conscience of a Generation* by Jeffrey Meyers (2000). It was the first biography to take advantage of all the new material in Peter Davison's 20-volume *The Complete Works of George Orwell*. Then, on the one-hundredth anniversary of Orwell's birth, came Taylor and Bowker's books, as well as a slim paperback biography by Scott Lucas. There's been nothing new since, apart from John Sutherland *Orwell's Nose: A Pathological Biography* (2016). But evidently this isn't a brand new biography with new material, more of a reinterpretation of the existing literature, from the angle of Orwell's interest in smell.

Then there's the original material by people who knew Orwell and left a record of their friendship. Rayner Heppenstall was first off the mark with *Four Absentees* (1960), quickly followed by Richard Rees, *George Orwell:*

Fugitive from the Camp of Victory (1961). Next came the memoirs assembled by Miriam Gross in her anthology *The World of George Orwell* (1971). This was followed by George Woodcock's *The Crystal Spirit* (1967), Jacintha Buddicom's *Eric & Us* (1974) and T. R. Fyvel's *George Orwell: A Personal Memoir* (1982). Two years later it was 1984, the excuse for a surge of publications. I don't have the time or the energy for all the academic critical-interpretation stuff (people cranking out their Ph.D. theses and all that jive). But I do want to read *Orwell Remembered*, edited by Audrey Coppard and Bernard Crick, and *Remembering Orwell*, compiled by Stephen Wadhams. These are collections taken from radio and TV interviews with people who knew Orwell.

This lot will see me through my first Ronnieless winter.

The Blair family arrived in Southwold in 1921 and lived at 40 Stradbroke Road. Everyone agrees about that except for Jeffrey Meyers.

In *Orwell: Wintry Conscience of a Generation* Jeffrey Meyers doesn't mention Stradbroke Road at all. He says that when the Blairs arrived in Southwold they went to live at 20 South Green. But he gives no source. But then again, I notice that nobody supplies a source for the Stradbroke Road address either. And, oddly, no one else mentions the South Green house at all. This is *seriously weird*.

I go and take a look at 20 South Green. It's a tiny house in a prime part of town, part of a terrace of four houses facing inland across the lush green open space named South Green. South Green is the most prominent of the Greens of Southwold, at the end of the main street. It's by a narrow passageway called Primrose Alley, which leads to the seafront.

Did the Blairs ever live here? The house looks smaller even than number 40, which was downsizing for the Blairs, who in their Henley-on-Thames days had a large detached house with an acre of land.

This is another mystery I need to solve.

What isn't in doubt is that when Orwell returned home in 1927 after five years in Burma his parents and sister were living at 3 Queen Street. This was a much posher house, a three-storey property with a complicated architectural history. Outside it looks Georgian but inside it's older. Its finest feature is the large living room with Jacobean wall panelling.

Today it's a holiday home available for weekly rentals and weekend breaks. The website lets you roam around the rooms and see the panelling. It even mentions Orwell.

Holiday lets are a hot topic in Southwold, though. Over half the town now consists of second homes and holiday houses. Local workers can't afford to live here anymore.

When I go for a haircut the woman who does my hair tells me she drives in from Lowestoft every morning.

I notice the impact when I go for an evening stroll. On street after street the houses are all in darkness. There's nobody here.

It's only at weekends or on sunny day-tripper days that the town comes alive. But the houses on either side of Vancouver Cottage stay empty and unlit, even at weekends.

I'm getting to know the pebbles on this beach. It's personal. I visit them every day. Hello, beach. It's just you and me.

Every day it's different. Some days the shingle is hidden by a layer of sand. Next day the tides have sliced off the sand and it's back to banks of shingle.

I never realised pebbles came in so many varieties.

There are the famous hag stones, the small lumpy uneven ones which have holes that run all the way through. They are dark-coloured, mostly brown or grey. You find them at low tide, close to the edge of the sea. At weekends I see people looking for them, then whooping with excitement when they find one. They aren't easy to spot and some days you don't see any.

My favourite ones are the Matisse stones. That's my name for them. Blue pebbles with patterns like wind-torn scarves, cut of a deeper blue. They remind me strongly of Nice and the Matisse collection there. That was the year when Timmy knew someone with a yacht. Our set were invited on a trip to the South of France. We spent three nights in the harbour at Nice. Three days of partying and eating seafood and making love under the stars.

I slipped away to see the paintings up the hill. It was only a ten-minute taxi ride. Ronnie wouldn't come. She was wearing a thong and nothing else. She was working on her tan.

A head and neck suddenly break the surface of the rocking waves. Sleek and black. For a split second I think it's a dog (labradors like swimming). Then I realise it's a seal.

Almost at once the creature dips down and vanishes. I walk on, watching intently for it to surface. But it stays down and I don't see it again.

I remember reading somewhere that seals can stay under for twenty minutes or more. They can swim a quarter of a mile underwater before they surface.

I'm wasting my time hoping for another sighting. I walk on, as far as the harbour. I walk as far as the chandlery.

And then I go back to George Orwell.

He's always there, waiting for my return.

*

Jane Morgan, the daughter of Orwell's older sister Marjorie, remembered her childhood holiday visits to her grandparents' house in Southwold.

Grandmother and Aunt Avril took breakfast in bed, one at the head and one at the foot. Earl Grey tea, toast and Patum Peperium. The dachshunds usually sat on the bed, which delighted and scandalised us.

Patum Peperium? I look it up on the net. It's another name for Gentleman's Relish. This is some sort of anchovy paste, mainly used to spread on toast. A popular delicacy in the 1930s.

Orwell remained addicted to Gentleman's Relish for the rest of his life.

Meanwhile there's a hurricane in the Caribbean, the window-panes are rattling in the upstairs bedrooms, and this year's winner of the Nobel Prize for Literature has just been announced. It's one of those years when I discover that though I think of myself as a reasonably well read and cultured individual I've not read a single book by the winner. Even though the name is well known.

Another gap in my knowledge.

On social media someone sarcastically lists previous winners of the Nobel Prize who now aren't read by anyone much. The list includes Theodor Mommsen, Frédéric Mistral, Selma Lagerlöf, Paul von Heyse, Henrik Pontoppidan, Władysław Reymont, Sigrid Undset, John Galsworthy, Roger Martin du Gard, Pearl Buck, Frans Eemil Sillanpää, Eyvind Johnson, Harry Martinson, Camilo José Cela, Elfriede Jelinek and J. M. G. Le Clézio.

(No, me neither...)

They won but Our Indignant Social Media Commentator – who goes by the name of Fiesta F. Fictu (eh?), hiding behind a pseudonym, just like Eric Arthur Blair – lists some of the writers who didn't get the Nobel Prize. They include Franz Kafka, James Joyce, George Orwell, Jorge Luis Borges and Vladimir Nabokov.

George Orwell. That name again...

Towards the end of his life he wrote: 'In reality there is no kind of evidence or argument by which one can show that Shakespeare or any other writer is "good".'

Not even Shakespeare? But surely Shakespeare is still read and his plays are still performed over four centuries after his death...

That line of argument won't work with Orwell.

'Ultimately,' he wrote in his 1947 essay on Tolstoy and *King Lear*, 'there is no test of literary merit except survival, which is itself an index to majority opinion.'

Orwell received only one literary prize in his life. In September 1949 the New York magazine *Partisan Review* awarded him their $1,000 annual prize for literature.

It was the only recognition he ever received as a writer.

Four months later he was dead.

I am buying half a dozen Cox's orange pippins in the little corner grocery shop in the marketplace when I suddenly notice it on a shelf. Some white circular containers bearing two familiar words: Gentlemen's Relish.

Oh. My. God.

It still exists!

I buy some, to try it.

Hmm... Yes, it's, ah, *interesting*.

It's got a very strong, distinctive taste. Vaguely, well, *estuarine*.

Use sparingly.

An acquired taste – like Marmite.

Somehow I don't think I'm going to become an addict, like George.

4   Going After a Ghost

TODAY I'M GOING AFTER a ghost.

The one that Orwell saw.

Yes, really.

George Orwell once saw a ghost. That's what he told his friend Dennis Collings, the doctor's son. He described it in detail in a letter dated August 16, 1931.

Orwell was twenty-eight, then, and completely unknown. He wasn't even George Orwell. He was still Eric Arthur Blair, unpublished wannabe writer. No job, no prospects. Hanging out with mum and dad in Southwold. Generally regarded in Southwold as a bit of an oddball. A lanky layabout.

He was in Walberswick, which is the village next to Southwold, the other side of the River Blyth. The village church is built inside the ruins of a much grander church, which fell into neglect when the local wool trade collapsed and the harbour silted up. Orwell describes how he was sitting there at 5.20pm on a July evening when he became aware of a figure walking past. A figure seen out of the corner of his eye. A small, stooping man, dressed in lightish brown clothes. The man disappeared behind some masonry and it then occurred to Orwell it was odd that the man hadn't made a sound. When he followed the man out through a doorway into the churchyard he found that the figure had vanished. He looked inside the church but the only two people inside bore no resemblance to the mystery figure.

Orwell provides his friend with a sketch of the churchyard, identifying where he was sitting and the path taken by the ghost. Then, at the end of this detailed account of what the reader can only assume *was* a ghost, Orwell remarks: *Presumably an hallucination.*

But Orwell wasn't the kind of guy who ever hallucinated. He never experimented with drugs. He didn't drink to excess. He didn't have mental health issues. He wasn't suffering from extreme thirst or hunger or mental and physical exhaustion. On the contrary. He was young and fit and sitting inside a ruined church in the lush Suffolk countryside on a pleasant July day.

That remark about the ghost having to be an hallucination is surely a defence mechanism. He was barricading his experience against possible mockery and sarcasm from his friend, who was a level-headed anthropologist.

The church inside the ruined church is still there today. So I'm off to examine the scene of Orwell's ghostly experience... Maybe I'll see the ghost too.

It takes less than an hour to walk there from Southwold. And that's at an easy pace. I'm in no hurry. I have, as Louis Armstrong once sang, all the time in the world. A song which always makes me think of Ronnie...

But the past is past. You can't stay there. You must move on, keeping pace with the restless, jerking hands of the clock.

I stroll across the Common to the two water towers, then cut across the golf course, through a patch of scrub and gorse and emerge by a fingerpost. I follow the sign which points south, down the old route of the railway. It leads in a straight line across the flood plain of the River Blyth, all the way to the bailey bridge. This provides a crossing of the Blyth for pedestrians and cyclists.

To the east the harbour moorings begin – a line of rickety structures with PRIVATE: KEEP OFF notices attached to gates which lead to narrow wooden piers. Most are empty but a few in the distance have yachts moored alongside. Beyond the yachts, on the Southwold side, are a few scattered buildings. There's no one in sight, apart from a distant woman with a dog.

West of the bridge the river broadens out into a wide, curving estuary framed by grass-covered mounds, which are flood defences. The surrounding plain is an expanse of ditches and reeds and empty fields. The brick torso of a windmill-shaped structure without sails rises up beside a distant flood defence. In the empty fields there are groups of swans, lying belly-down on the grass.

I suddenly notice a heron.

It's standing by the edge of the river two hundred yards away, completely motionless. Its beak points down at the brown slow-moving current. When I reach the far side of the bridge and the old railway embankment beyond it becomes nervous of my presence and abruptly rises and flaps gracefully away upriver.

For ten minutes I follow the line of the old railway to a point where a single-track tarmac road swerves away to the left and the footpath continues. There's a bench with a plaque, beside a rectangle of cracked, overgrown concrete.

The plaque states that this was once the site of Walberswick railway station.

Which means that George Orwell was once here, sitting in a carriage, staring out at the surrounding countryside, while passengers climbed aboard and white swirling steam drifted past the window from huffing-puffing Thomas the Tank Engine.

It was the most eccentric railway service in Britain, running on track with a tiddly one-yard gauge. There was one section of track where it struggled to get up a small rise. Sometimes the passengers had to get off to let it continue.

Orwell first used the service in 1921 and continued using it until he left for Burma in the fall of 1922. It was still there in 1927, when he returned. But when he came back from Paris at the end of 1929 he discovered that the line had shut down. Competition from omnibuses had put the company out of business.

Instead of following the line of the old railway, which plunges on through a gorse-covered common, I turn off to the left, following the single carriageway tarmac track into Walberswick.

Gorse and briars billow up on all sides and I continue along this green tunnel until I reach the outskirts of the village.

The road widens out and big detached houses appear, looming beyond high dense yew hedges and clumps of trees.

I come to the main street that runs through Walberswick and turn right. The church is just a few minutes walk away, now.

Soon it comes into view, next to the road. According to my research this road is called 'The Street'. Very original, that...

The Church of St Andrew runs parallel to the road. Over the low pebbled stone wall I can see ancient graves dotted around an expanse of freshly mown grass. The ruins of the older church dominate the newer, smaller one built in its shell.

I walk in through the little gate and head between the graves for the ruins and the place where Orwell saw his ghost.

It's easy enough to locate the exact site, using Orwell's sketch, which was included in the letter to Dennis Collings.

Everything's just the same.

This is where Orwell saw the apparition. It glided across the open space behind him and was lost to view behind the wall to his right. The figure could only have gone through the ancient priest's door – which then as now is simply an open space – and out into the graveyard beside the road.

But it must have been different in 1931. Orwell was surprised that the figure made no sound as it passed but that wouldn't be a surprise today, as the floor of the ruined church is velvet-soft grass. No one walking here today makes any noise. In Orwell's day there must, by implication, have been stone or gravel coating the floor of the old chancel.

Orwell identifies the place where he was sitting inside the ruins. But there's no bench here now and there probably never was. Today it's just open space and grass. Was Orwell sitting cross-legged on the grass? The logical place to sit would be not on the grass but on the low stone wall which forms the lowest part of the frame of the huge, long-vanished south window.

None of this is making any sense.

Orwell claimed it took him twenty seconds to follow the ghost out into the graveyard, only to find it empty. But I don't understand why he felt he had to walk across the chancel and through the priest's door. From where he was sitting he could have simply stepped over the low wall and into the graveyard. He didn't need to waste time following the path taken by the ghost when he could have taken a far more obvious short cut.

In any case it doesn't take twenty seconds to get from where Orwell was to the priest's doorway. If I hurry it takes ten seconds, if I saunter it takes fifteen. But Orwell was surely moving at speed on those long, lanky legs of his. He could have been at the priest's door in under ten seconds if he'd really thought he was pursuing a ghost.

If Orwell took twenty seconds to get to the churchyard then that gave the man time to go into the church, or even walk round to the tower. Orwell says he went into the church but he doesn't mention questioning the people who were there.

In any case there are places out of bounds to visitors. If the guy was a workman and not a ghost he might have gone up the stairwell to the tower.

Conclusion: Orwell was simply flexing his narrative muscles. The tale he told Dennis Collings was an exercise of the imagination.

Besides, I don't believe in ghosts – apart from Orwell's.

And round here that's everywhere.

So I follow Orwell's ghost through the priest's doorway, out into the churchyard. And as I glance towards the church porch my heart stops – then races.

There's a figure in the churchyard, a few yards beyond the porch. A woman wearing blue jeans and a dark coat. She has strikingly red hair, cut very short.

I've no sooner absorbed her presence than she's moved beyond the porch, out of sight.

I don't make Orwell's mistake. Never chase a ghost directly. Approach it from an angle.

Instead of hurrying the full length of the two churches to catch up with her I turn back and go across the soft grassy open space of the old chancel. I walk quickly beside the north wall of the new church and out through the priest's doorway at the far end of the ruins. This way I'll meet the Orwell girl face to face.

Thirty seconds later I'm standing at the foot of the tower.

And she's not there.

She's gone.

But where?

Grinning gargoyles look down at me with slice-of-melon chins and malice in their dark, diamond-shaped eyes.

I walk round to the far side of the tower.

The churchyard is empty.

I go inside the church.

There's no one. The silence here is total. It's a bright, airy church, filled with light. Not remotely spooky.

Where in hell can she be?

I'm sure there's a perfectly natural explanation. I go round one side of the church, she goes in the other direction the other way. We are destined never to meet. It's pure chance. So it goes.

Or maybe she had a taxi waiting for her. She took a quick picture of the church tower then strolled across to the driver waiting by the church gate and was whisked away.

I go back outside. The clocks changed to winter time the other day and now already the afternoon is starting to thicken, with a faint dusky texture in the sky. The distant woodland is beginning to go a little blurred.

I didn't bring a torch with me.

I need to get back to Southwold before nightfall.

5   Harbour Inn

A TIDE OF DENSE, milky mist spreads across the marshes and the river's flood plain. It reaches the old railway embankment and lies at its base like a strange, congealed flood. The path to the river ahead of me stretches in a straight line to the bridge.

On the bridge is a dark figure, motionless by the railings.

The sky is a lurid mackerel pink, ribbed with layers of mauve cloud.

As I get closer I see the person on the bridge is a woman. As I get closer still I see she has a crop of short lurid red hair.

She doesn't seem to notice me striding towards her along the embankment.

I feel like I'm in a painting by Caspar David Friedrich. Two figures in an empty landscape, with mist rising like smoke.

The conical outline of the old wind pump cuts through the mist like the conning tower of a submarine.

She is standing on the bailey bridge, staring down at the river. For a second I have the strange and terrible feeling she's about to jump.

But no one would hurl themselves off this bridge. It's only a few feet above the surface of the river, which is not very deep here. Plunge into this river and you'll find yourself landing on a bed of soft mud.

I reach the bridge and there's no mistake. It's the Orwell girl.

I'm starting to think she's a figment of my imagination. In a moment she'll pop like a soap bubble.

She remains motionless, like that time I saw her at the end of the pier. Intent, concentrating her gaze. Lost in her own private intensity.

I walk towards her, feeling a slight tremor under my feet. The bridge seems shaky, like a suspension bridge. She must surely be aware of my approach but she doesn't turn and glance at me.

I get close and see her profile. She has a snub nose, an intense gaze, a small, slightly protruding chin. Serious but pugnacious.

When I'm almost level with her I say: 'George Orwell once dropped a pair of field glasses here.'

'Yes, I know,' she replies. 'They were Brenda Salkeld's. He went down and waded in to retrieve them. The water was waist deep. He found them.'

She finally twists round and looks coolly at me. 'So you see, mister, you aren't telling me anything I don't already know.' Her tone is combative.

She has fierce green eyes, a silky golden skin and – the biggest surprise of all – *she's American*. Her accent is West Coast, marinated in sunshine. That explains her smooth perfect skin, tinted by years of bright Pacific light.

I can't help laughing at her criticism. 'That puts me in my place,' I acknowledge. 'But then again I suppose I should have guessed you'd know all about Orwell.'

I tell her about seeing her photograph Montague House; how the memorial tablet to Orwell whetted my appetite to know more about his Suffolk years.

'In fact, I've just been to Walberswick to check out the churchyard where he saw the ghost.'

Now it's her turn to smile. 'Yeah, I thought I saw you there. Plus taking a dip at Easton Broad. Imitating Orwell there too, eh?'

'So it was *you*!' I cry. 'I had a weird feeling someone was there.'

'Yeah, Big Sister was watching. But only by chance.'

I want to say: *And did you like what you saw?* But I don't. Instead I ask: 'On holiday?'

She says she isn't, not really. It's more to do with work.

And then we talk a little more before agreeing to head for The Harbour Inn for a drink.

The Harbour Inn is just a few minutes' walk away, along the riverside path. We pass by rotting jetties and big silent moored yachts with no one aboard.

The path meets the harbour road which cuts across the Common and the marshes. This road turns sharp left to follow the river and here there's a wide area of rough ground where people park to visit the Inn. But today there is only a handful of cars. The lights of the Inn glimmer in the puddles which dot the gravel car park.

I push the door open. We step into a large saloon bar which is empty apart from a huddle of fishermen at the far end. They glance up, stare at us, then revert to their beers and conversation. Stairs lead up to other drinking areas and I follow them until we reach a smaller bar at the top of the Inn. There's no one here, so we occupy a corner table in a quiet nook and I go and get some drinks.

There are nautical flags pinned to the ceiling and photographs of the old harbour on the wall. Uneven timbers, blackened by time, cross the ceiling. This place is seriously old.

I'm disconcerted that Paige will drink only mineral water. Women who don't drink always make me nervous. But she insists. She needs to keep a clear head, she says. *For what?* I wonder.

I return with a couple of menus, her bottle of Spa water and a half of dry hopped lager. After we've sorted out the food and I've ordered, we talk.

Her name is Paige Yapor (rhymes with 'vapour'). She teaches cultural studies at a university in Los Angeles. She's on sabbatical, with a scholarship to finance the book she's writing: *Orwell's Women*. It's basically a feminist critique of Orwell and his representations of women, combined with a biographical study of his friendships and romances. I quickly learn that her heroine is Eileen O'Shaughnessy – Orwell's first wife. Eileen was feisty and, Paige reckons, far more radical than Orwell. She probably wrote some of *Animal Farm*. And the marriage went sour, which was Orwell's fault, not Eileen's.

Paige is also a fan of two other women in Orwell's life. The first is Brenda Salkeld. She was the gym mistress at St Felix School for Girls here in Southwold. Orwell was besotted with her from the moment he met her. He was twenty-five, she was twenty-eight. Like him, she was exceptionally tall and slim. She was a virgin. Orwell lusted after her for years. She told him she was considering taking a lover. But she didn't fancy him – not physically. Orwell was terrific company and she liked going for long walks in the countryside and talking about books. But she didn't want him pawing her, let alone – the horror, the horror – sexual intercourse.

Orwell's revenge was to write *A Clergyman's Daughter*, which is what Brenda was. The clergyman's daughter, Dorothy, is a repressed virgin who resists all attempts on her honour. She won't even accept an offer of marriage, even though it would rescue her from a life of drudgery. The novel also includes 'Miss Foote, a tall, rabbit-faced dithering virgin of thirty-five'. Brenda was tall and thirty-four.

The other woman is Mabel Fierz. She was an older married woman Orwell met on Southwold beach. Mabel's husband had a tennis partner who was a literary agent: Leonard Moore. When Orwell was in despair after five years of trying to become a writer and suffering multiple rejections it was Mabel who bullied Moore into reading his work and taking him on. Within a year Eric Blair had reinvented himself as 'George Orwell' and his first book was published. Without Mabel Fierz, a strong woman, we might never have heard of George Orwell.

I remember reading all about Mabel in Gordon Bowker's biography. That's the best one for Orwell's sex life. (One of Bowker's competitors sniffs that where Orwell is concerned Bowker 'leaves no woman unturned'). Orwell wrote to her in London, saying he was coming down from Southwold to the capital and maybe they could go for a decent walk in the countryside.

Naughty Mabel retorted that she'd prefer to go for an indecent walk with him.

Paige breaks into laughter. Yes, she knows that story too. As she laughs she puts her hand lightly on my knee. Mabel. Quite a woman. A tough cookie.

Paige has that ebullience which seems part of the American DNA. I can't help comparing her to Ronnie. Whereas Ronnie was very tall and very slim with a chiselled face and high delicate cheek bones, Paige is much shorter, with a fuller, more rounded body. Paige seems vital and fresh and bubbly, whereas Ronnie always talked in a slow, languid drawl, in a manner that always seemed faintly redolent of a kind of debauched exhaustion.

I suddenly realise I'm thinking about Ronnie in the past tense.

Paige's small hand rises from my knee like a butterfly and flutters into the air to sketch more of Orwell's biography.

She's telling me she's in Southwold pursuing the ghosts of four Orwell women. There's his mother Ida Mabel Blair (another Mabel!) and sister Avril Nora Blair. Plus Brenda the formidable gym mistress. And last of all, Eleanor Jaques. Eleanor who did what Brenda wouldn't...

Orwell often brought Brenda to The Harbour Inn. They used to go hiking across Walberswick common, then call in on their way back to Southwold. Sometimes they'd hire horses for the day and go out riding in the woods. Brenda remembered that when they came here they always booked a private room. By the sound of it they both wanted to get away from the rough types who drank here in the days when the harbour was a busy commercial port packed out with trawlermen and visiting sailors. In those days there was a branch of the railway which ran down alongside the river. Ships used to unload coal. The place hummed with activity.

In their private room at the Inn the couple talked books. Nothing more.

There are no private rooms at the Harbour Inn nowadays. I'm wondering if the small quiet bar where Paige and I are sitting used to be the place where Orwell and Brenda came. It seems more than possible.

Later, after our potted shrimps and salad, we walk back into town. Paige tells me she is staying at an Airbnb on Pier Avenue.

We walk along the narrow road that leads up to the two water towers. It's now night but the sky is clear and moonlight casts a silvery light on the silent road.

The bigger of the two water towers is illuminated by floodlights. It's a vast Art Deco structure on tall slender concrete supports which make it look like some kind of giant insect. The older, smaller pepper-pot water tower lurks in its shadow like a child. They both existed in Orwell's day. So much of Southwold is the same, architecturally, as it was one hundred years ago. That's part of the town's charm.

We pass the entrance to the golf club, where Orwell's father was club captain for three years in a row. Impressive. His name is supposed to be on a board inside. I tell Paige I'm going to walk up there in the daytime and ask to see it.

'I'll come with you,' she says, smiling.

'But that's nothing to do with Orwell's women,' I reply.

'Yes, it is, mister. It's a symptom of the sexism back then. Brenda played golf. So did Orwell's mother. But *ladies* were never allowed to hold positions of responsibility at the club.'

I shrug. She's right, of course.

We walk on in silence.

We reach the High Street. I offer to walk her to her accommodation but she says it's not necessary. The streets are well lit and Southwold, notoriously, is a place where nothing happens. The last reported crime was the theft of a dog bowl outside a bakery.

I give her my phone number. She doesn't give me hers.

We stand face to face. I nod farewell.

'Call me,' I say.

'Sure.'

But she doesn't. Not the next day or the day after that or the day after that.

6   Mandalay

WHEN SHE DOESN'T PHONE I go out for walks, restlessly searching the town, looking for her. Each time I go I make a long diversion so that I walk the entire length of Pier Avenue, wondering which house she's staying in. I even walk up and down it at night, staring in through lighted windows, hoping to see a figure inside with blazing red hair. But there's no sign of Paige Yapor. No sign at all.

I begin reading *Burmese Days*.

The hours pass.

I go online and look up the website of the university where she works. There she is: red-haired, snub-nosed, honey-skinned, with an expression which is half pugnacious, half merry.

Her eyes hold a sparkle. *Life is a joke*, they seem to say. *But, hey – let's take it as it comes.*

I patrol the beach, all the way from the sea defences north of the pier to the entrance to the River Blyth.

At the harbour I chat to one of the few remaining trawlermen, who is sitting next to his moored ship wrestling with a tangle of fishing net. He tells me he's lived here all his life. He fills me in on some local history. The caravan park used to be the coal yard. The site of the old octagonal fish market is now occupied by the public lavatories.

I walk back over the belt of sand dunes which runs between the river and Gun Hill. And here I make an interesting discovery.

The formidable Mabel Fierz recalled the first time she ever met Orwell when she was interviewed for a TV show, half a century ago.

We met him at Southwold. We had a little cottage on the beach. He'd been in the habit of sketching from there. And he turned up one day with his painting brushes and his colours, and he said, 'I'd no idea that this place had been let. I've been in the habit of sketching from here.' So we said, 'Oh well, don't let that worry you, we shall be very pleased. Come whenever you like.' Which he did.

A little cottage on the beach...

They still exist, these holiday homes on the beach. There are nine in all. Once they were fishermen's huts. Then they were transformed to something rather more substantial. No planning laws back then. At the harbour end there are six small properties on the beach. Then there's a gap, then there are three more, marooned among the dunes and surrounded by rabbit holes.

One of these is an old wooden chalet painted bright blue. It has a small fenced-off front yard with a balcony. It was surely here in the 1930s, when Orwell first encountered Mabel. I can just imagine him coming to this particular property to sketch and paint. It's more isolated than the others and it looks out over the sand and the sea. The perfect spot for an artist...

It's just a private fantasy – but then I spot the name. This property is called 'Mandalay'.

That clinches it. Mandalay was where Orwell first went in Burma. He lived there for a year, training to be a police commander. One of the volumes he had to study was the *Manual of Map Reading and Field Sketching*.

Coming to 'Mandalay' to sketch would have appealed to Orwell's acute sense of irony.

I can't wait to tell Paige.

Assuming I ever see or hear from her again...

I can't stream anything on my grandmother's archaic television, so I'm reduced to DVDs.

I buy the DVD of *Keep the Aspidistra Flying* from Amazon and watch it the day it arrives. It's a gentle version of the novel, which exposes the weakness of the original text. The hero, Gordon Comstock, is intolerably egocentric, weak and selfish. Why would his girlfriend (Helena Bonham Carter) bother with such a tedious and repellent individual?

Answer: I've known lots of lovely women attached to slobs. It's real life, Benjamin.

Why would his friend and patron Ravelston (Julian Wadham) also bother?

The actor playing Ravleston seems familiar. I look him up on IMDB. He was in *The English Patient*. And *War Horse*. And some other movies and TV dramas I've seen.

Richard E. Grant as Gordon Comstock is wonderful. He looks half-crazy. He's perfect for the role. And he's tall like Orwell and dresses like him. Flannel trousers held up by a belt, way above his navel. Sports jacket, shirt, tie. His mad staring eyes, wildness.

This reminds me I should watch *Withnail and I* again. I haven't seen it for years. I remember getting Ronnie to watch it. She didn't like it. She wrinkled her elegant nose. She shuddered and called it *grubby*.

Hey, *Keep the Aspidistra Flying* stars Harriet Walter! That's a bonus. I adore Harriet Walter. And she's perfect for the part, too. The sister, working in a tea shop. Harriet Walter is tall, like Avril. As Comstock's sister she's probably too downtrodden to be much like Avril though.

Avril was a tough cookie, is my impression. But I need to find out more about the sister Orwell was closest to.

Paige will know.

It's stupefyingly hot, has terrific storms and heavy rain, and the country is controlled with violence, repression and a vast network of informers. A bit like Tudor England, then, only with worse weather.

Burma.

None of Orwell's biographers ever went there and who can blame them? It's not what you'd call tourist-friendly. It's one of those *everything's broken and no one speaks English* places. Yes, it's even worse than Italy or Wales...

The Burmese speak multiple languages, according to their ethnicity. And now it's not even called Burma. The army changed it to Myanmar. They've also banned *Animal Farm.* The army is worried that people might read it and somehow get the impression it's about Myanmar. Which of course it is, although it was never planned that way. Books sometimes hold meanings that become apparent only long after their authors are dead.

The Burmese have an Orwell joke. Orwell, they say, having spent five years in their country, was inspired to write a trilogy about it: *Burmese Days, Animal Farm* and *Nineteen Eighty-Four.* But don't let anyone from Military Intelligence hear you telling that joke. Because if they do you'll be hauled off to the Ministry of Love and beaten up or tortured.

But the army don't mind *Burmese Days.* That book's fine with them. Which is not a tribute to its critical perspicacity, even though – roll of drums and blast of trumpets – George Orwell's best novel is *Burmese Days.*

Okay, it's not his most important novel – that's obviously *Nineteen Eighty-Four* – but as literary fiction it's his best. It's beautifully crafted. It has a wide range of very believable characters and is tightly plotted and atmospheric. It offers a dark satire on an outpost of the British Empire. And best of all is the style. It drips with style. Every sentence sings. For one book only, Orwell played at being Flaubert.

Orwell claimed that he wrote two novels after coming back from Burma, neither of which found a publisher and both of which he destroyed. My guess is that one of them was an early version of *Burmese Days*. When he began writing it – or rewriting it – he spent far more time on the book. In the end it dragged on over several years. He had plenty of time to think the book through and polish the words until they glittered. And the style was perfect for a book set in a hot, sultry exotic location. *Burmese Days* pours over the reader a luscious treacle of adjectives. At times I'm reminded of Nabokov or Updike.

And for Orwell fans there's now an essential appendix to the book, in the form of Emma Larkin's *Finding George Orwell in Burma*. Ms Larkin went on the Orwell trail in the last decade of the twentieth century. She was the first person to do so since Orwell departed from that country seven decades earlier. And she found stuff which had eluded all Orwell's biographers.

The biographies give the impression that Orwell was largely deskbound as a colonial policeman. Not so, asserts Emma Larkin, who has delved among the India Office papers at the British Library. Orwell went out into the field – or rather the river. She followed in his wake, in a canoe. She also went to all the places where he was stationed, finding old, mouldering colonial houses. And she made some amazing discoveries. In Moulmein, where Orwell's mother Ida Limouzin grew up, she discovered a street named *Leimmaw-zin*.

Perhaps the single most amazing moment in the book is when she investigates an old Anglican church in Moulmein, where the caretaker shows her a collection of old gravestones rescued from the town's main cemetery. One of them is an ancient slab of black marble. As the dust is wiped away the words ELIZA EMMA LIMOUZIN appear, died 1865, aged twenty-three. She was the first wife of Orwell's grandfather, Frank Limouzin.

There's only one surviving picture of Frank.

It's a studio portrait.

He looks grim, wild, even a little angry. And he seems to be having a bad hair day.

Nobody really knows what Orwell got up to in Burma. He was remembered as a rather aloof individual.

His life probably wasn't anywhere near as eventful as the plot of *Burmese Days*. Lives are never as neat as novels. Maybe that's why we read novels. They compress the important things in life and give them structure and meaning. Whereas lives are always messy and shapeless, with lots of loose endings.

Those vast three-decker Victorian novels are a ripping read. But they are false to what was going on at the time and wedding-bells endings don't convince anymore.

Maybe contemporary fiction needs to be fragmentary in form. To mirror the atomised, speeding nature of our days...

7 Lost Love

THERE'S A CLUE TO Orwell's state of mind in Burma in his letter to Brenda Salkeld, sent during his long hot miserable summer of 1934. At the Southwold cinema they were showing *The Constant Nymph*. Orwell told Brenda he had no intention of going to see the movie – soppy, drippy sentimental stuff – but he remembered vividly the novel. He said he'd read it when it came out, when he was about 23, and he found it so moving he almost wept.

That would date his reading of the book to 1926, when he was based in Moulmein, or possibly (because Orwell's dates are a contradiction – *The Constant Nymph* was actually published in 1924) earlier, when he was based at Insein.

Insein had a prison, which was where Orwell probably witnessed a hanging. It's pronounced 'insane'.

Either way his emotional response to Margaret Kennedy's hugely popular book provides a clue to the inner Orwell when he was alone in Burma.

I'm getting a little frantic, now. It's been five days and Paige hasn't phoned. And she seems to have vanished from Southwold. I walk the streets at all hours and never see her. I know every house on Pier Avenue.

I give up searching.

In a charity shop in the High Street I find a second-hand copy of *The Constant Nymph*. I shut myself away with it.

The title, from a modern perspective, seems a bit weird. That word *nymph*. I can't help but associate it with *Lolita*.

By the end of the novel I understand the title's meaning. Margaret Kennedy doesn't mean 'constant' in the sense of 'regular' or 'perpetual'. She means it in the sense of 'faithful' and 'loyal'.

The nymph is the book's young teenage heroine, Tessa. She's the daughter of Albert Sanger, a great composer who lives in exile in a chalet in the Austrian Tyrol. At the start of the novel Sanger is visited by one of his admirers, Lewis Dodd, an accomplished young musician and composer. Tessa, aged fourteen, is deeply in love with Dodd but never tells him. (Lolita, remember, was twelve.) After Sanger's death Dodd becomes infatuated with Tessa's older cousin, Florence. They marry and return to England. There, Dodd discovers that his marriage was a mistake. Florence is far more conventional and controlling than he had ever realised. Too late, he recognises that his perfect mate is Tessa. They flee to Brussels. Finally they are alone together in a room with a double bed. But before they can make love for the first time, Tessa dies. For a long time she has been suffering from a valvular lesion but has bravely kept this terrible news from Lewis.

Her shockingly unexpected death leaves the other principal characters having to face up to the consequences of her sudden absence from their lives.

It's a weepie. No wonder movie-makers loved it. It was filmed in 1928, 1933, and 1943. It was a smash-hit play. It was a bestseller. It's still in print today. (Respect.)

What made it so popular?

At first I found the novel a bit stodgy but then it picks up pace and I start to get interested in the characters. But the setting is flimsy – I'm not really persuaded that Margaret Kennedy had ever been to Austria. If she had, her landscape descriptions are curiously flat and one-dimensional.

It's a very old-fashioned novel (James Joyce would also have wept). Kennedy dips in and out of her characters' minds. She's an omniscient, all-controlling narrator. The motives and feelings of everyone in the novel are laid bare and analysed.

But there are alpha pluses. This is a novel about music and musicians and I've never read a book which so atmospherically expresses the experience of hearing music.

It ends in the restaurant of an expensive hotel in Brussels, where a band is playing some ballet music by Sanger. Lewis cries out, 'I shall forget her.' Florence, victorious over her now dead rival, anticipates the challenge which her marriage now faces:

> To go on living, to be confronted every day with the necessity of thinking, to look forward into the empty years and make plans for them, to build up upon wrecked love a monument of worthy achievement, this seemed to her a much harder thing.

So in the end it's a deeply romantic novel. It suggests that people never end up with their one true love. Instead they accommodate themselves to the wrong partner and to the world around them. They go on through life, surviving heartache. It's a novel, finally, about endurance. And novels are part of the furniture of survival. They console us with their stories. They get us through the night.

The popularity of *The Constant Nymph* indicated a world full of broken-hearted readers. But then it was published just seven years after the First World War. Britain was full of bereaved women. The nation was wounded.

And in 1925, in hot Burma, who was Orwell weeping for? Himself, obviously.

His great lost love was Jacintha Buddicom.

As a teenager Orwell had been great friends with Jacintha, her sister Guinever and her brother Prosper. By the age of eighteen he had fallen in love with Jacintha, who was two years older. She was bookish, like him. But Jacintha wasn't interested in romance or marriage. One of his love poems grumbled, 'My love can't reach your heedless heart at all'. Jacintha retorted by advising him to turn away from love's bright dangerous dazzle: 'It's best/To rest/Content in tranquil shade'.

Jacintha was small and slim with big sensuous lips and hair that fell to her waist, like a woman in a pre-Raphaelite painting. In the summer of 1921 she was twenty years old. Orwell fancied her like mad. He wanted her. But Jacintha had no intention of surrendering her virginity.

He departed for Burma the following year, still regarding her as his one true love and prospective wife. Once out there he wrote her a long letter which she described as 'very disconsolate'. Burma, he said, was awful. She briskly, sensibly, crushingly replied, saying 'if it was as bad as that, hadn't he better leave and come home?' He wrote two more letters, which she ignored. But he remained infatuated with Jacintha and still regarded her as his prospective wife.

When Orwell returned in 1927 he brought with him an engagement ring. But Jacintha avoided him. He gave up his long pursuit of her, stopped contacting her family, and never saw her again. Then, two decades later, on Tuesday February 8, 1949, Jacintha Buddicomb received a letter from her Aunt Lilian telling her that 'George Orwell' was her old friend Eric Blair. Next day Jacintha telephoned Secker and Warburg, who obligingly gave her Orwell's address (that wouldn't happen nowadays, would it?). By now he was seriously ill with pulmonary tuberculosis and in The Cotswold Sanatorium, Cranham, Gloucestershire. She wrote to him and they began a short correspondence. He urged her to come and visit. But her nerve failed. She had a terrible secret she couldn't bring herself to confess. Their correspondence fizzled out. Then, suddenly, he was dead. She turned up for the funeral service and sat at the back. Nobody knew who she was and she was ignored.

After his death Jacintha couldn't stop thinking about Orwell. She'd turned him down twice in her younger days, and rejected him a third time when he requested that she visit him at the sanatorium. He'd told her about the death of his wife Eileen, and his adopted son, who now desperately needed a mother.

She could have been Mrs Orwell, the wife, then widow, of a world-famous writer...

But no, I don't think so.

She wasn't Orwell's lost soul mate. If he'd married her in 1921 or 1927 the marriage would surely have been a disaster. Whatever they had in common as teenagers, Orwell became a very different person as an adult. Jacintha, on the other hand, remained a prissy and deeply conservative woman – as her reactions to his published work reveal.

As soon as she learned that 'George Orwell' was really her old friend Eric Blair she rushed to read his books.

She began with *Down and Out in Paris and London*, which 'very much disconcerted' her.

She didn't like *The Road to Wigan Pier*, which seemed 'inclined to pull cockroaches rather than plums out of the pie'. She shared her acquisitions with her mother. The two women read Orwell's books 'with increasing bewilderment'.

The Buddicom family politics were plainly not Orwell's: 'By *Homage to Catalonia* I was shocked'. Jacintha plainly had a soft spot for that blood-spattered fascist brute General Franco, judging by her scandalised response to Orwell's participation in the Spanish civil war. 'It is impertinence,' she huffs and puffs, 'for independent members of a different nationality to interfere with the internal affairs of a country not their own.'

Things just got worse. 'By the other novels we were more baffled still.' But the basis of her critical analysis was nothing more than nostalgia: 'it was difficult to relate their author with Eric'. Eric had been such a nice boy. He'd appeared 'admirably balanced'. Whereas the works of George Orwell were, well, horrid and beastly and often rather unpleasant...

But while she was deploring his books in the company of her old mother, she was still writing to Orwell. She wondered if he would like her to send him some jigsaw puzzles.

OMG!

Jigsaw puzzles!

'Thanks awfully for the offer,' he diplomatically replied. But actually he was pretty well supplied with materials to pass the time. So: *No.*

Nineteen Eighty-Four was published on June 8, 1949.

On Saturday June 11 Jacintha travelled from Chelsea to Shiplake to spend the weekend with her mother, who had been reading the new George Orwell novel. She dourly informed her daughter it was 'very morbid'. The book's nightmare world and defeatist vision 'upset her very much'.

Jacintha said goodbye on the Sunday evening. In the early hours of Tuesday she was telephoned with the news that her mother had died from a fatal heart attack.

It would be unreasonable to suppose that *Nineteen Eighty-Four* killed her mother, Jacintha wrote. But perhaps not *that* unreasonable, she insinuated. Her mother 'was very frail indeed when she read it, and it certainly did not make any happier her last few days of life'. Privately, in a letter, she accused Orwell's book of provoking her mother's fatal cardiac arrest.

Jacintha claimed to recognise herself in the novel. It's heroine, Julia, she insisted, was all too plainly intended to be a representation of *herself.*

She had to endure *the public shame of being destroyed in a classic book.*

Orwell, the bastard, had not only killed her mother. He'd also torn her 'limb from limb in public'.

WTF?

Jacintha's indictment seems to combine vanity with delusion and paranoia.

When *Nineteen Eight-Four* was published no one thought for a moment that it was autobiographical or contained characters based on real people. It was a novel set thirty-five years in the future.

There were no complete Orwell biographies until 1980, some thirty years after his death. And, although it is now recognised as a very personal book which did indeed include portraits of people Orwell knew, no one for a moment thought that Jacintha Buddicom, of whom little or nothing was known, was the model for Julia.

She quite plainly wasn't. Julia is promiscuous and hungry for sex – quite the opposite of the Jacintha Orwell knew.

Most critics believe that Julia, if based on anyone, is a portrait of Sonia Brownell, who became Orwell's second wife. 'Memories of Sonia – her youth and prettiness, her toughness, above all her radiant vitality – fed directly into the book's heroine,' wrote Hilary Spurling in her biography, *The Girl from the Fiction Department.*

After Orwell's death Jacintha wrote two memoirs of her

old friend Eric. The first one appeared in 1971 in a handsome volume of essays edited by Miriam Gross, *The World of George Orwell.*

She wrote how she knew Eric Blair very well for seven years. He was one of the most interesting, best informed, considerate, thoughtful, kindest and *nicest* boys she knew. For example, when he gave her a copy of *Dracula* for Christmas he thoughtfully included – how sweet! – a small crucifix and a clove of garlic (difficult to obtain back then in Henley-on-Thames).

He was *so very nice* in those days it was impossible to connect him to those horrid books he wrote in later life: 'the novels of George Orwell baffle me'.

I can well believe that.

When *The World of George Orwell* was published Jacintha was furious. 'They edited out most of the important bits,' she grumbled. But unfortunately not the two execrable poems in memory of Eric which she modestly slotted into her essay...

In 1972 Orwell's first biographers, Peter Stansky and William Abrahams, diplomatically described Jacintha's short essay as 'a charming memoir' which testified to the young Orwell's 'essentially happy life away from school'. Miss Buddicom, they recognised, 'saw a good deal of him' in his younger days.

And Orwell saw a good deal of her – although *not as much as he wanted to.*

It would be another thirty-four years before the steaming, malodorous truth emerged from behind Jacintha's fragrant smokescreen.

Publication of her truncated memoir inspired her to pen a much more substantial reminiscence, and in 1974 there appeared *Eric & Us: A Remembrance of George Orwell*.

Clever Jacintha!

She managed to outwit and mislead every single Orwell biographer from Bernard Crick (1980) all the way to D. J. Taylor (2003).

One of her chapters was entitled – *phwooaar!* – 'Eric and Sex'.

It was teasing clickbait.

Eric, she piously insisted, had no romantic interest in her at all. As for sex: it was never discussed, let alone practised.

'He never made any attempt to seduce me,' she told one interviewer.

In the summer holidays of 1921, just before the Blairs moved to Southwold, Mrs Buddicom and Mrs Blair and their children jointly rented a house at Rickmansworth. '1921 was a gloriously, unforgettably, hot summer, immediately brought to mind whenever we hear the tunes of the day.'

I'm Forever Blowing Bubbles.

The Stephanie Gavotte.

Auguste Durand's *Chaconne, Op. 62.*

And some long-forgotten minor hit called *The Chinese Wedding Procession.*

Unforgettable. And yet, strangely, Jacintha suddenly couldn't remember the last time she saw Eric before he went to Burma. And – amazing coincidence – 'No more of Eric's letters are extant for that year'.

And when Orwell wrote in anguish from Burma: 'Before I got round to writing, the letters were lost and I couldn't remember the address.'

And when he came back after five years abroad?

Sadly, alas, 'completely unavoidable circumstances' prevented her from seeing him.

After that he completely disappeared, and none of us heard a word from him. So we had no idea that he had changed his name.

Ms Buddicom, who never married, was muddying a lot of water.

Born in 1901, she died in 1993. Thirteen years after her death her memoir was republished, with a devastating postscript by Dione Venables.

It contained two explosive revelations. Firstly, at the end of that long hot summer of 1921 Orwell had attempted to rape Jacintha. He'd ripped off her knickers and tried to penetrate her. She screamed and fought back and finally he stopped. She ran back to the house, sobbing, bruised, with her skirt torn. Everything Jacintha Buddicom had written about her relationship with the teenage Eric Blair was false. She was in denial, both about his romantic infatuation with her and his assault.

Secondly, she concealed the fact that she held off her male admirers until the end of the summer of 1926. It was only then, at the age of twenty-five, that she finally surrendered her virginity to an Oxford friend of her brother's. She became pregnant, at which point her lover abandoned her and fled abroad.

In May 1927, just before Orwell got back from Burma, she gave birth to a daughter. The reason she avoided him upon his return was her sense of shame. She felt sure he'd reject her. The baby was passed on for adoption to a childless aunt and uncle. Orwell never did find out the truth.

Jacintha Buddicom: the first Orwell girl.

But, in the end, the least important one.

8   Celery, Bogart, Golf and Beds of Moss

MY PHONE STARTS RINGING. A shrill, nagging sound.

It's Paige.

She wants to meet me by the water towers on the Common tomorrow morning at ten.

I say Yes.

Yes, I will, yes.

What was George Orwell like?

'He always looked pale and a little bit withdrawn,' said his Southwold tailor, Jack Denny.

'He's like a long, long, very clean stick of celery,' said a landlady, Mrs Saddell. 'Take him away and scrape him!'

Mrs Saddell sounds like she wandered out of a Dickens novel. I really have no idea what she means by that scraping remark. Why would anyone want to scrape a length of clean celery? Surely you only scrape celery when it has soil embedded in the fibres?

And this is the curse of an obsession. Now when I see the bags of celery in a supermarket I think of George Orwell and Mrs Saddell.

O.M.G.

I've just discovered that there's a movie of *Homage to Catalonia*.

I never knew that and I'm a big movie-goer.

Says Jeffrey Meyers:

Ken Loach's *Land and Freedom* (1995), loosely-based on *Homage to Catalonia*, portrays an idealistic English Communist in the Spanish Civil War and his bitter disillusionment when his side is betrayed by the Stalinists.

A quick check on Amazon shows that it's still available on DVD.

I order a copy.

Meyers suggests that the script of *Casablanca* owed something to Orwell.

In the movie Humphrey Bogart asserts that the United States is not prepared for war, when it urgently needs to be: 'I bet they're asleep in New York. I'll bet they're asleep all over America.'

That's a Hollywood replay of the last sentence of *Homage to Catalonia*: 'sleeping the deep, deep sleep of England, from which I sometimes fear that we shall never wake till we are jerked out of it by the roar of bombs.'

I stand by the copse at the back of the two water towers, staring across the empty common. It's five to ten and there's no sign of Paige.

Half a dozen gulls drift by overhead. On the far side of the deserted rugby pitch there's a woman walking her dog.

But no Paige.

I made a special effort to be here on time. I glance at my watch. There's still two minutes to go.

'Let's go, mister,' an American voice says right behind me, making me start. I whip round to encounter her smile, her merry, marble-green eyes, her faintly pugnacious expression.

'Call me Ben, please. Not mister.'

'Sure thing, Mister Ben.'

I gesture towards Southwold. 'I was expecting you to come that way.'

'I was down by the bridge. Now, let's go.'

A magical mystery tour. Where are we going? Paige doesn't say.

She sets off past the towers, down the road to the river. I don't ask what she was doing by the bridge. Instead I say: 'I thought I might see you around town this past week.' I don't say: *I've been walking the streets, looking for you everywhere.*

'I've been away.'

'Away?'

'In London. At the Orwell Archive at University College.'

'Ah.'

'But now I'm back. I decided to finish my book here. I prefer it to the big city. It's quieter. I get more done.' She turns and looks at me: 'No distractions.'

The gorse bushes press close on both sides of the road, big billowing clumps of dark impenetrable greenery. The branches are wiry and twisted, like the arms of a very old and thin person.

'We're here,' she says.

A sign says SOUTHWOLD GOLF CLUB.

We walk up a short drive. The club house comes into view – a low, single storey structure.

The entrance door is open. We go inside. A florid-faced man wearing an argyle cardigan is standing in the lobby, holding a pair of irons.

His face registers a flicker of shock at the proximity of a woman with blazing red hair. The momentary horror deepens when Paige speaks. This woman *isn't English.*

But then he crumples in the face of her warmth and confidence. Paige says she has the permission of the club secretary to see the Captains' Board. She explains the Orwell connection.

'It's right here,' the man gruffly replies, pointing at the wall with his free hand.

Paige cries, 'Oh my God! Look, Ben!'

She finally called me Ben.

And sure enough, there it is. The name of George Orwell's father, Richard Walmesley Blair, beside the designated years of his captaincy, 1925-1927, when Orwell was in Burma and turning against everything his father believed in.

We walk back up towards the water towers.

Once we've passed them Paige plucks at my arm.

'No,' she says. 'Not Southwold. There's another place we need to take a look at first.'

She steers me north, across the Common.

Magical Mystery Tour, phase two.

Down and Out in Paris and London was Orwell's first published book. His author's copies were delivered to Montague House, Southwold. It was published two days after his father's seventy-sixth birthday. It marked the climax of five years of effort to become a writer.

When he'd returned from Burma and broken the news that he was going to be *a writer*, not even Orwell knew what kind of writer. At first he thought he'd be a poet. But he was hopelessly out of touch with the ferment in contemporary poetry. T. S. Eliot, Ezra Pound and E. E. Cummings were ripping poetry apart and reassembling it. Orwell's heroes were Rudyard Kipling, Hilaire Belloc and G. K. Chesterton – fusty late Victorians who wrote jingle-jangle verse irrelevant to the Jazz Age.

Orwell left the glacial interior of 3 Queen Street, Southwold, and went to London. But after six months in London, he'd made no impact on the literary world. London was full of wannabe poets. He headed for Paris. There, he finally started getting work published. But it was humdrum reviewing work. Nobody was interested in his poetry or his fiction. He wrote two novels. Both were turned down by every publisher he submitted them to. He destroyed them. But he kept a diary of his life in Paris. And there were three slabs of experience which he carried away with him to reconstruct as prose.

The first was his experiences on the Rue du Pot de Fer, where he rented a room. This was a narrow, scruffy street in central Paris lined with six-storey tenements. It was home to drifters like Orwell himself: students, White Russian exiles, North Africans. It was cheap and cheerless. Here Orwell encountered the colourful characters he displayed in the first part of *Down and Out*. A rich, Dickensian cast of desperadoes, living on the edge. Every one of them had a story and, quite probably, Orwell grafted some of his own failed fiction onto the tales they had to tell. Ultimately *Down and Out in Paris and London* is an anthology of short stories – it's just that they purport to be true. But when the book was published, Orwell sent a copy to darling Brenda of Bedford. He annotated it, admitting that it wasn't as authentically autobiographical as it purported to be. It had been altered and re-arranged in all kinds of ways. Some of it was based on hearsay. At the beginning of the third chapter Orwell scribbled: 'Succeeding chapters not actually autobiography, but drawn from what I have seen.' A tautological formulation...

In February 1929 Orwell went down with pneumonia. Feverish and unwell, he ended up in the Hôpital Cochin. It was a free hospital which supplied medical students with a continuous stream of impoverished patients to practise their skills on. And if there were blunders and mistakes – well, the poor were in no position to protest. Orwell carried the scars of this experience with him for years. It was only in 1946 that he published an account of this searing experience, 'How the Poor Die'. And when he emerged from hospital and had recovered, his money ran out. He spent two months as a *plongeur* (dishwasher) in a high class hotel, and then a restaurant. This provided him with good copy about the squalor behind the glamour. The cook spitting in the soup. The waiter running his fingers through his oily hair, then dipping them in the gravy. The dropped chicken returned to the diner's plate...

The second half of the book – the accounts of nights in casual wards and the company of tramps – describes episodes in England which occurred before he went to Paris. But they aren't as colourful, and it was a shrewd editorial move to place them after the good stuff.

At the end, Orwell writes: 'I had made friends with an Irish tramp named Paddy Jaques, a melancholy pale man who seemed clean and decent.' Their friendship was brief but Orwell believed 'he was a typical tramp'.

But Orwell never did know an Irish tramp called Jaques. Instead he knew a local Southwold woman named Jaques. Remember her from page 27? When she was a teenage girl Eleanor Jaques lived on Stradroke Road, Southwold, at the same time as the Blairs at number 40.

In the summer of 1932, while he was putting the final touches to the manuscript of *Down and Out in Paris and London*, Orwell was romantically pursuing Eleanor. The biographers explain that by now the Jaques family had moved to the village of Reydon, just outside Southwold, where they lived at a house called Long Acre.

Which is where we're heading.

Paige shows me a photocopied section from an old map of Reydon, with Long Acre marked. It's beside the Wangford

Road.

Street networks tend to endure for centuries, especially in a place like sleepy sluggish Suffolk. We cross the Common and emerge by the site of the old railway station. Today there's nothing but a modern building and a plaque.

We walk north, out of town, along the road that crosses Buss Creek and the marshes. We pass the neat flowerbeds and the village sign at Reydon Corner and then turn right at the next junction, up a sloping road lined with large detached houses half-hidden behind billowing hedges. The old housing turns into new housing and an open area of grassy land comes into view: *Jubilee Green*. Beyond it is the village's only hotel, The Randolph. It's a big mock-Tudor structure with large clear windows – *Good prose is like a window pane* – through which can be seen an empty restaurant and drinkers in a parallel bar. The hotel was here in the 1930s, when Paige's map was produced. So we're almost there...

Except we're not.

Now there's a house which is obviously only a few years old and a street sign which reads **Long Acre** and underneath **Cul de Sac**.

We turn in and check it out.

The narrow driveway curves round to a small estate of a dozen new houses, grouped around the access road.

Long Acre must have been demolished, with new housing built where the house and grounds were.

I remember reading that after Eleanor Jaques died a cache of Orwell's letters were discovered at Long Acre in a box marked *Destroy when I am dead*. But her husband, Dennis, did not destroy them. He contemplated publishing them as a short booklet. A blunt letter from Sonia Orwell warned him off. He might own the letters but she owned the copyright. They ended up in *The Collected Essays, Journalism and Letters*, edited by Sonia and Ian Angus.

But Sonia censored the letters. For example, in a letter to Eleanor Jaques written in the spring of 1932, Orwell wrote that he might spend the summer in Southwold. He needed to get on with his novel *Burmese Days*, as well as a poem he was writing. He was thinking of going to some quiet place in France *where I can live cheaply & have less temptation from the World, the Flesh & the Devil than at S'wold.*

Sonia missed out the next sentence: *You can decide which of these categories you belong to.*

Eleanor would have understood. She was a keen churchgoer and Orwell's theological reference to temptation derived from the Anglican Book of Common Prayer: *From all the deceits of the world, the flesh and the devil: Good Lord deliver us.*

Eleanor responded swiftly and warmly to his overtures.

'She was a flirt,' I say to Paige, as we turn away from Long Acre and walk back towards The Randolph, discussing Eleanor Jaques and the tramp's surname in *Down and Out*.

'That's unfair,' Paige retorts, eyes flashing. 'She was indecisive. That's an altogether different thing.'

Orwell's next known communication with Eleanor was a handwritten lettercard postmarked Thursday 18 August 1932, sent from his parents' new Southwold home in the High Street. Lettercards were single sheets of paper which, once the message was written, were folded up; the sender then sealed it before posting. This lettercard indicates a major change in his relationship with Eleanor Jaques. Gone is the stiff formality. Now she is 'Dearest Eleanor' and the card is signed 'all my love/Eric'. He writes to confirm an assignation the following Tuesday at 2.15 pm outside W. H. Smith's in Southwold, adding 'as you love me, do not *change your mind* before then'.

In 1932 the W. H. Smith's store in Southwold was situated at 1 Station Road, on the corner with Blyth Road, having relocated there from the railway station when the train service ceased three years earlier. It was a good place for a discreet rendezvous, being a short walk from the Jaques family home in Reydon and an even shorter walk for Orwell. It was at the edge of town, where fewer local gossips were likely to spot them, and Southwold Common was just a few yards up the road. Beyond the Common lay the harbour and the river, and beyond the river was Walberswick.

The name 'Walberswick' partly derives from 'Berige', meaning 'a hiding place'. It was appropriate to what occurred there between Orwell and Eleanor that summer.

What happened is indicated by his next known letter to her, written in mid-September after his return to Hayes and teaching. Referring to the recent change in the weather – unpleasantly wintry – Orwell recalled the excellent weather they had enjoyed together in Southwold. He added:

I cannot remember when I have ever enjoyed any expeditions so much as I did those with you. Especially that day in the wood along past Blythburgh Lodge – you remember, where the deep beds of moss were. I shall always remember that, & your nice white body in the dark green moss.

Sex.

Final written proof that at the age of twenty-nine George Orwell had finally had sex. It might even have been his first

84

time. True or not, that day in the woods with Eleanor haunted Orwell to his final days.

There's an argument among Orwell's biographers about whether or not he used prostitutes. Later. Not today; not now. It's too nice a day to spoil it with mud, slime and shadows...

'Let's go for coffee,' I say, and Paige nods: 'Sure.'

We turn into The Randolph. Apart from three men at the bar the place is empty. It's still too early for lunch.

The bar is a big, bright room, filled with daylight. We settle down at a table by one of the windows.

'I'm still looking for Blythburgh Lodge,' Paige informs me.

No search engine mentions it. Maybe it's also been demolished. And Orwell's biographers don't know where it is either. They're all vague when it comes to identifying the spot where Eleanor stripped off her clothes and lay back on the dark green moss. The standard version is along the lines of *One day during a walk in a wooded area near the River Blyth, they made love.* But vague stuff like that tells you nothing. The River Blyth runs in a straight line past Southwold harbour, all the way to the bailey bridge. It's framed by embankments. There's no woodland. After the bridge it swerves to the west and broadens out into a wide estuary edged by open farmland. Again, no woods. The only place where the woods get close to the estuary is The Heronry. But there's no lodge anywhere near and never was.

'Maybe the lodge was demolished.'

Paige shrugs. 'Yeah, maybe.'

'In which case we'll never know where Orwell fucked Eleanor Jaques.'

Paige rests her hand on my arm. 'Let's not give up yet. Let's keep looking.'

I reach into my pocket and bring out my copy of *The*

Constant Nymph.

'Cool,' she says. She picks it up and turns it over. She laughs, reading the blurb. 'The era when women defined themselves by their husbands,' she says, pointing to the author description: *Margaret Kennedy is the wife of His Honour David Davies, Q. C., Commissioner for National Insurance.*

I hadn't really noticed that. But then I'm a man. My optics still require constant adjustment.

The Constant Nymph is an example of what Orwell wrote about in his essay 'Good Bad Books'. A good bad book is a work of popular fiction which remains readable when more serious literary work has lost its readership.

The supreme example, wrote Orwell (in 1945), was *Uncle Tom's Cabin.* It is implausible, melodramatic and ridiculous. It is also deeply truthful and touching.

A bad example, really. Does anyone really bother reading *Uncle Tom's Cabin* nowadays?

'I read it,' Paige says. 'Long time ago. It was better than I expected.'

But you can see what Orwell was getting at.

John Buchan is still highly readable in the twenty-first century. The prose of Erskine Childers' *The Riddle of the Sands* is as fresh as if it were written yesterday. But nobody bothers to read John Galsworthy, who in his lifetime was a literary giant. Or for that matter J. B. Priestley. Or, more recently, Angus Wilson. And Iris Murdoch is surely ebbing away...

Richard Rees, who was one of Orwell's closest friends, suggested that *Nineteen Eighty-Four* was itself a good bad book. It's seriously flawed but its merits outweigh its defects. It will still be read, Rees pugnaciously argued, when the works of the over-rated James Joyce have slid into obscurity...

Hmm...

We stay at The Randolph for a light lunch. I wash mine down with a pint of Adnams but Paige shakes her head at alcohol. A Coke's fine. She has writing to do. She can't work with a fuzzy head. Even one glass of wine will make her drowsy, she says.

We eat and talk. And talk and talk the Orwell talk.

'I brought you a present,' she says. 'From London.'

She passes me a photocopy. It's something she came across in the Orwell archive at UCL. His application form to join the Indian Police Force.

I take it and glance at what Eric Arthur Blair has written.

'Wow!'

'That's right.'

'So the Blair family *did* live on South Green. And they were living at number 20 by April 1922 – which means they weren't at 40 Stradbroke Road for more than a few weeks.'

Paige nods.

'Which means the Blairs had *four* addresses in Southwold, not three. And all the biographies are wrong!'

'Got it in one, buster.'

'We're making history, baby.'

'Don't exaggerate. We're making a minor adjustment to the existing record.'

I drain my glass and shrug. 'Whatever.'

I can't help feeling elated.

Afterwards we walk back into Southwold. On the corner where Orwell met Eleanor Jaques outside W. H. Smith's we part. Paige gives my hand a squeeze, bobs forward and plants a quick kiss on my cheek. Then she walks away.

I stand and watch her go. She must sense I'm watching

her because without looking back she raises her right arm and gives a wave.

I head off up Station Road. I come to a modern block of buildings called Crick Court and smile. It's impossible to get away from George Orwell. Crick was the name of Orwell's first biographer, Bernard Crick, author of *George Orwell: A Life*. 'The definitive biography', shouted the *Sunday Times* when it was first published, back in 1980.

Orwell's widow Sonia didn't agree. She hated the book and regretted ever asking the Professor to take the project on. She even tried blocking its publication but discovered she had no legal grounds to do so.

Others disliked the book, but from a perspective different to Sonia's. As a biography it was felt to be an arid document which evaded the central issue of Orwell's personality. 'Crick's biography,' wrote Michael Shelden, 'is a large collection of facts which relies heavily on the notion that facts speak for themselves if presented in enough detail.'

Crick, Sheldon suggested, reduced Orwell to nothing more than *a dry functionary*.

A furious Crick retorted that 'there are too many dishonest, flash biographers, striving for effect, not truth'. He meant Shelden, who wrote what he himself modestly described as *The Authorised Biography*. Authorised by the agent acting for the Orwell estate – not really a *magisterial* authorisation...

But later Orwell specialists have largely agreed with Shelden. Jeffrey Meyers wrote that Crick had made no attempt to understand Orwell's inner life. In his opinion Shelden's was 'a better biography'. John Sutherland has described Crick as a biographer who regularly poured buckets of cold water over any attempt imaginatively to go beyond the cold hard facts.

Crick also comes across as pompous and prickly. After Crick's biography was published, W. J. West came across sixty scripts and broadcasts by Orwell which had been lost in the BBC archives. This had been missed by all his biographers. But Crick was less than gracious in acknowledging this interesting discovery. West, sniffed Crick, 'describes himself as a scholar and bibliophile' – with the clear insinuation that he was an inferior species to Bernard Crick, of the London School of Economics, Harvard and Birkbeck College. The interpretation which W. J. West placed on this goldmine of new material was, Crick sneered, obsessive. West had lost 'any sense of proportion'.

Crick was also less than gracious in acknowledging the pioneering biographical work done by Peter Stansky and William Abrahams. In *The Unknown Orwell* they had made one small error in describing The Hawthorns, where Orwell briefly taught, as a prep school. Crick is ecstatic in his correction of this trivial error, thundering that 'The Hawthorns did not prepare the pupils for university matriculation but for the examination of the Senior College of Preceptors (acceptable in commercial offices for salaried and pensionable clerical work).'

There's also a lengthy footnote attacking Stansky and Abrahams for other minor errors relating to The Hawthorns. It's all strongly reminiscent of the student thesis-writer, who sprays criticism on everyone else in the field and who modestly presents his or her self as the first person truly to understand the subject.

In reality Stansky and Abrahams were far better biographers than a dullard like Crick. They wrote two pioneering accounts of Orwell's early life in the face of hostility and obstruction from both Sonia Orwell and the

Orwell estate. Their understanding of Orwell seems to me spot on and far superior to a heavy lumbering rhinoceros like Crick.

I walk on and turn right into York Road. Almost at once I come to Orwell Court – a block of apartments.

The author or the river?

Frankly, I couldn't give a damn.

9   Not Waving

7PM.

Lights twinkle on the pier and in the opposite direction a distant green light shows at the end of the harbour wall.

Paige raps on the brass anchor-shaped knocker and I let her in. Vancouver Cottage has a wood-burning stove and the living room is cosy and warm and filled with the orange flicker of burning logs. A Jimmy Yancey album is tinkling quietly in the background.

'This is so cute!' Paige seems thrilled by small rooms and low ceilings. I show her around. She stares out from my bedroom window overlooking the dark ocean. She spots the green light at the harbour, half a mile or so away down where the beach ends at the river. 'Oh my God, this is so like *The Great Gatsby*,' she shrieks, pressing her little hands together and whooping delightedly.

Back downstairs I attend to the cooking. It's a simple meal and when it's ready she joins me in the kitchen. While I'm cooking she's been looking at my piles of Orwell books.

'Awesome,' she says.

But she means my cooking rather than my library.

And neither is, particularly. I've whipped up a bog standard spaghetti bolognaise with a packet of mixed salad from the local convenience store, plus a wholemeal loaf from the High Street artisan bakery. The only thing that's really truly awesome is the wine – a dusty bottle from granny's cellar. It's a twelve-year-old Bourgogne Rouge. A wine bore would say it has lashings of character.

Paige agrees to have a glass.

Thank God.

I was beginning to fear she might be a fervent teetotaller.

Later we watch the movie, which is the reason she's

called round.

1984, the first film version, released in 1956. The DVD jacket reproduces the original poster, which shrieked WILL ECSTASY BE A CRIME – IN THE TERRIFYING WORLD OF THE FUTURE?

It's a clunky black and white adaptation, which uses the American title. For some reason no one ever got to the bottom of, the U.S. edition of the novel used numbers for the title, not words.

Some of the scenery is doubleplus good, filmed on location on real bombsites in London. Exposed cellars covered in weeds and the sides of shattered buildings create the sense of a city under bombardment. And *Nineteen Eighty-Four* is a novel which recreates Orwell's sense of living in London during the Second World War, with sticks of bombs laying waste to the centre and the suburbs. Then, later, the puttering V1 and the faster, more devastating V2.

1984 begins where *Dr Strangelove* ends, with atom bombs exploding and rising mushroom clouds. It cuts to a voiceover explaining how the world became divided into three warring superpowers. Then the camera zooms in on London, capital of Airstrip One. It's a model, with futuristic buildings resembling the modern-day gherkin rising above an older, more recognisable city. I think I can see Westminster Bridge and County Hall – but the House of Commons has vanished.

A siren wails in an urban landscape of bombed-out buildings. Civilians flee to an underground shelter. A pack of security cops on motorbikes roar into the foreground like Hell's Angels and take up positions with their weapons. And Winston Smith comes running down the road, hiding in a shop doorway at the sound of nearby bombs. He emerges – only to run back there for shelter as more bombs land nearby. A woman dashes in and joins him, huddling close. It's Julia.

They gaze at each other – then Winston rushes away.

And this is the first of the film's problems. Casting. Edmond O'Brien is hopelessly wrong as the main character. Winston Smith is an emaciated, unattractive man with false teeth and varicose veins. But Edmond O'Brien is a big, fleshy, bull of a man. In 1949 he was voted the sexiest man in America by the Young Women's League of America – an organisation which sounds oddly Orwellian. But by the 1950s he was fighting a weight problem, and it shows.

Ditto Julia. Jan Sterling just isn't right for the role. She has short blonde hair and a rather weird face, with big, bulging eyes. In the novel Julia is freckled, black-haired and feisty.

Even the huge posters for Big Brother are wrong. BB is an ordinary-looking bloke with a slightly receding hairline. Not remotely scary.

As for the screenplay. Oh dear. The complexities and subtleties of *Nineteen Eighty-Four*'s themes are boiled down and reconstructed as sugar lumps.

Don't you see? There must be others like us in love, who will rebel! All I know is when we're together it's wonderful to be alive!

Quick – pass the sick bag.

There's zero chemistry between O'Brien and Sterling. And because this is the 1950s there's no nudity. Their relationship is comprehensively sanitised. You'd never know that Julia is crazy for sex and has had scores of lovers. You'd never know that Winston Smith has dark rape fantasies and is turned-on by Julia's scandalous sexual history.

It gets worse. There's an orchestral score which ranges

from boisterous to jaunty and it won't go away. In every bloody scene there's an orchestra in full flow in the background. It's far too lively and intrusive. *Nineteen Eighty-Four* should be a movie where the true soundtrack is rats scuffling and scratching behind walls.

Jan Sterling's undistinguished career as a movie actress faded. By the real year 1984 she was a forgotten figure from a vanished age.

Edmond O'Brien enjoyed far more success. But he barely made it beyond 1984. By that year he was incarcerated in a Sanatorium, suffering from Alzheimer's Disease. When he became violent and aggressive he was put in a straitjacket.

By a hideous irony he ended up in the real 1984 in the same condition as his character in the movie – held back by restraints, howling in terror.

He died the following year.

'That's creepy,' says Paige, when I tell her.

And, like me, she's not too impressed by the movie. 'What bugs me is that they changed O'Brien's name!'

She means the character in the novel. Because the film production used the actor Edmond O'Brien, they changed the name of Orwell's Thought Police character O'Brien to O'Connor.

'They shouldn't have done that. And they should have got a thinner actor.'

Paige finishes her second glass of wine. She puts the glass down and hugs her knees to her chest. She looks lost in thought. Finally she says: 'I was trying to think of who Edmond O'Brien reminded me of. And now I've remembered. He was a dead ringer for George Kopp.'

And then she looks at her watch and says she has to go.

She lets me walk her back to her apartment. We take the cliff-top path to the pier. To the east is a vast darkness, apart from the lights of an anchored ship far out at sea. Southwold is sunk in silence and the streets are empty. When we reach East Green the beams of the lighthouse swing by overhead. Everything seems magical and somehow we're now walking hand in hand.

And Paige is talking about Kopp. *George Kopp.*

When Orwell went to Spain he ended up fighting in the Lenin Division. His commander was George Kopp – a big man with an even bigger back-story. He claimed to be a Belgian, a reserve officer and a widower. All lies. He was a maverick, a fabulist and a charmer. He seduced Orwell's wife, Eileen. He later married her sister-in-law's step-sister. A ladies man. George Kopp. Sometimes spelt Georges. Or Jorge.

We linger outside the dark house where Paige is renting the top floor apartment. There's no one in the other two below.

'I'm spending the next two days writing,' she says.

'Let's meet when you're done,' I say.

'I'd like that.'

She gives me a quick kiss and a hug and then unlocks the door and goes inside.

Next day I find it.

After hours online, searching links that lead to links, I finally come across a website that shows part of an old Ordnance Survey map of the Walberswick area. On it, west of the town, is clearly marked Blythburgh Lodge.

The elusive house that Orwell mentioned in his letter to Eleanor Jaques. The one postmarked September 19, 1932, in which he mentions never having enjoyed walks in the countryside as much as the ones with her, *Especially that day in the wood along past Blythburgh Lodge.*

The wood where Eleanor stripped off all her clothes and lay down on the moss and allowed him to fuck her. A moment that Orwell reprised in *Nineteen Eighty-Four*.

The wood no Orwell biographer has ever identified, because no Orwell biographer has ever located Blythburgh Lodge.

Hey, guys! I found it!

Woo-hoo!

Some Orwell mysteries will never be solved.

Take, for example, the case of the poet Stevie Smith, whose immortality rests on that much-anthologised poem, 'Not Waving but Drowning'.

During the Second World War, Orwell formed part of the capital's literary set and the two became friendly. She sent poems to him at the BBC to be broadcast.

The big question is, *how friendly*?

Orwell girls always fell into two categories: those who would and did and those who wouldn't and didn't. It was a long-established pattern. Jacintha Buddicom wouldn't and didn't. Eleanor Jaques would and did. Brenda Salkeld wouldn't and didn't. Kay Welton would and did. Sally Jerome wouldn't and didn't.

And Stevie Smith?

In a collection of poems published in 1942, at the time she knew Orwell, she wrote a poem about *bliss* which has the lines:

I like to get off with people,
I like to lie in their arms,
I like to be held and tightly kissed,
Safe from all alarms.

Next to the poem she placed a drawing of a couple having

sex outdoors, while a strange animal watches them.

What's this got to do with George Orwell?

Nothing – or perhaps everything.

In his autobiography, the novelist Anthony Powell describes how Orwell once asked him, 'Have you ever had a woman in a park?' The social-climbing, luxury-loving Powell winced and said: No. Orwell explained that he *had*, because there was nowhere else for him and the woman to go.

Malcolm Muggeridge also remembered Orwell boasting over lunch of fucking in a park. And Orwell always liked al fresco sex. It was a turn on. The sensation of cool air on one's skin, the wide sky above, the sense of smashing bourgeois conventions and, perhaps, the extra thrill of being observed... In the manuscript of *Nineteen Eighty-Four* Orwell describes the Thought Police watching and filming Winston and Julia as they copulate in the room above Mr Charrington's shop. But then he had second thoughts and deleted the description. Too close to the bone...

Friends lined up to confirm or deny the theory. Stevie Smith's friend Norah Smallwood remembered her confessing to *an intimate relationship* with Orwell, which *wasn't easy*. Which it wouldn't have been, bearing in mind that he had a wife and was also fucking other women at the same time. And Stevie famously shared a house with the woman she called her Lion Aunt, who was always there, observing, criticising, scowling. Perhaps the strange animal in Stevie's little drawing is a lion.

But others insisted that this could never have happened. But then again, what does anyone ever really know about another couple's sex life?

And now we'll never know for sure, one way or the other.

There's a photograph of Stevie Smith sitting on a bench in the garden of Clare Road, Cambridge, in the summer of 1938. She's thirty-five and unmarried. She's skinny and wearing a dress that rides twelve inches or more up her thigh. It could be a miniskirt and a snap taken in the swinging sixties. Her raised right hand holds a cigarette, in a carefree swagger. Her left hand rests over her crotch, just touching a book or a folder of poems. There's a tight, sharp smile on her face. She's faintly conscious of being photographed and faintly amused by the fuss.

And she's *hot*. She's unbelievably sexy.

Look closer and you'll see she's barefoot.

What red-blooded man wouldn't want to persuade this slender delicate merry-eyed poet to lie down on the grass and pull up that skimpy dress and part those slim long legs?

I'm reading *The Holiday*, the novel Stevie Smith wrote during those early London wartime years and couldn't get published. It took years to find a publisher and finally appeared only in 1949. The year that *Nineteen Eighty-Four* was published and the dying Orwell took to his hospital bed for the last time.

To be honest, I'm not enjoying it. *The Holiday* is basically a rambling monologue written in a deadpan faux naïve style with lots of repetition. Sentences like this one:

Everybody feels that he is cold and lost, said Caz, but not everybody will say as much, a lot of people will say that it is very jolly and will bite the people who say it is not; it is better that people should know that they are cold and lost.

It's also a *roman à clef* – a novel with a key. This is a minor genre which relies for its interest on extra-literary biographical associations. Caz is Stevie Smith herself, as is Celia, the narrator. Pearl is her sister Molly. Lopez is Inez Holden (another Orwell girl). And Basil Tait and Tom Fox are both versions of George Orwell. Basil is an old Etonian who has fought in the Spanish civil war. He's talkative, sceptical and opinionated, given to sweeping generalisations ('He said that America would be the ruin of the moral order'.) Tom Fox has a 'long mad stride' with 'something anarchic' inside him. He works at the BBC, where he makes broadcasts to China. He persuades Celia to go with him to the studio, where he takes her head in his hands and runs his hands down to her throat. The narrator confesses that 'Tom's madness stretched out and met in me something that was also mad, or rather – willing to be mad.'

A sentence which makes me think they did have a fling, Stevie and George.

The Holiday was revised for publication. It was a book written in wartime and it needed alteration to bring it up to date as a contemporary novel of the late forties. That gave it a retrospective detachment. 'I think of Tom,' says Celia, 'and wish for comfort I was in his arms again, and much comfort that should be, it is not in Tom's arms that comfort lies.' Which was a shrewd acknowledgement of the impossibility of any woman finding happiness with George Orwell. Impossible, egocentric Orwell. *He thinks that women are biologically necessary and resents the necessity*, says Celia of Basil. *He had the power to see a thing while it is yet a long way off*, adding: *but you cannot make a diet of salt.*

Stevie Smith reminds me of Eileen O'Shaughnessy. A

waspish wit. She had the measure of the man. And in the end Orwell damaged his beloved Eileen. Her marriage became one of quiet desperation and misery. It was redeemed by the adoption of a baby – a substitute for the love Orwell couldn't or wouldn't give her.

Paige agrees. She thinks Stevie Smith and Orwell really did fuck. Quite possibly only once, in a London park.

She also turns out to be a big Stevie Smith fan (which I'm not).

And she points out her favourite line in *The Holiday*, which had passed me by. It's the one where Basil Tait is summed up as 'like a fourteen-year-old boy you know, he thinks girls can't play'.

Southwold is behind us.

At the end of the path along the old railway embankment we pass the overgrown platform of Walberswick's long-vanished station. Here we follow the narrow asphalt-coated lane which winds over the Common to the village high street. I last walked this way on my way to the church to find the place where Orwell saw his ghost. Now I'm not alone. Paige bobs at my side, effervescent with conversation. She's in a good mood. Her book is getting near the end. She'll have no problem reaching her publisher's deadline.

She's amused by the bulk of my rucksack. It's because I've packed a picnic. Sandwiches, cherry tomatoes, goat's cheese, a crisp fresh baguette, a bottle of Sauvignon Blanc in a wine cooler. Plus a couple of French fruit tarts from a local deli. Plus in a cupboard at the cottage I found a groundsheet and a tartan rug. So we're sorted. And it's another unseasonable gorgeous hot sunny day. July in November. Global warming is kicking in. It makes me think of an old Gaelic sign which Ronnie and I once saw by the ruins of a castle when we were staying on an estate in Scotland. *The world may end*, it read, *but music and love endure.*

Paige says: 'That's pure poetry. It's so touching.'

'But it's not really true, is it?'

'Why isn't it?' Her eyes spark with indignation. I realise she wants it to be true.

'Because music needs musicians. And love needs people too. And when the world's ended all the people are gone.'

She says nothing. I see that my words have in some strange incomprehensible way upset her. Her eyes brim with tears.

'Hey,' I say. 'That's why we need to live every day as if it's the last one of our lives. The hell with tomorrow.' I take her hand. 'Onwards to Blythburgh Lodge.'

In Walberswick we turn off the main street, before we get to the church. There's a side road leading out of the village. Lodge Lane. Bordered by trees, it's a narrow dead-end road that rises up a low hill.

We make our way up it, through dappled light and shade. There are no cars: just silence and peace. We step across bands of blazing asphalt wherever the boughs part. Clouds of tiny insects swarm at shoulder height, parting to make way for us as we toil on up the slope. Under the trees to the left the ground is carpeted with yellow fallen leaves.

We continue on for twenty minutes, until the trees drop away and an expanse of green meadowland opens up. In the far distance are a rolling forest and the fringe of Dunwich marshes. Beyond that lies the pale dome of Sizewell nuclear power station – a huge, ghostly golf ball, incongruously landed in this place of rural tranquillity. The dying Orwell was convinced that atomic warfare would break out very soon, and it seems strangely ironic that a nuclear installation should end up on his old Suffolk doorstep. Among the junk mail lying on the doormat inside Vancouver Cottage that first day was a leaflet stating that, since Southwold lies inside the Sizewell evacuation zone, all residents are entitled to free iodine tablets in the event of a nuclear disaster...

'That's it,' I say, turning to point in the opposite direction, where beyond a high brick wall the turreted roof and top floor windows of an enormous house have come into view. The architecture looks Victorian. It reminds me of the houses you see in paintings reproduced on the covers of Wilkie Collins paperbacks.

'That's Blythburgh Lodge.' Or rather that's what it was called in Orwell's day. Today the name has been changed to Westwood Lodge, which explains why no Orwell biographer managed to identify it.

'It's so big. And so isolated.' Paige stares, wide-eyed. 'I mean, like, who *lives* here?'

I've no idea. Maybe a hedge fund manager. Someone who can afford to buy a mega-house with a ton of land in prime real estate country.

I did some research on the net but it didn't yield much. The chief fact of interest is that the Lodge is built on the site of the medieval manor house.

The asphalt road surface stops beyond the gate that leads to a side entrance to the house. The lane continues as a rough, uneven mud track studded with stones and dotted with potholes. We continue along it, the high brick wall to our right shutting out the house. Now all that's visible are the tips of tall, fluted mock-Tudor red brick chimneys.

Ahead of us, woodland closes in again around the little

lane, the ground on either side banked high and covered in greenery. This is the wood where Eleanor Jaques and Orwell wandered on a summer's day in 1932. Aptly, its name is New Delight and it's basically an outlying offshoot of Dunwich Forest.

> I cannot remember when I have ever enjoyed any expeditions so much as I did those with you. Especially that day in the wood along past Blythburgh Lodge – you remember, where the deep beds of moss were. I shall always remember that, & your nice white body in the dark green moss.

The implication that Eleanor's 'nice white body' was naked and that they'd had sex in this wood is confirmed by a letter Orwell wrote to her the following month, replying to one of hers. She'd evidently told him that she also remembered with pleasure their days out together that summer. His response was briskly utilitarian: 'I hope you will let me make love to you again some time, but if you don't it doesn't matter. I will always be grateful to you for your kindness to me.'

To the end of his life Orwell never forgot that summer's day. It resurfaced in the dying author's *Nineteen Eighty-Four* when Winston Smith and Julia have sex in the woods. Julia, the girl from 'the Fiction Department' is a composite figure. With her Anti-Sex League sash and wholesome appearance with its 'atmosphere of hockey-fields' she resembles Brenda Salkeld, games mistress of St Felix School for Girls. Brenda even made the long journey to the island of Jura off the west coast of Scotland to visit Orwell while he was writing the novel.

But the heroine of *Nineteen Eighty-Four* turns out to be

energetically promiscuous, and some biographers suggest that Julia was inspired by Sonia Brownell, the woman who became Orwell's second wife. Sonia – known in some quarters as 'the Euston Road Venus' and in others as 'buttocks Brownell' – achieved something of a reputation as a bed-hopping girl about town. In appearance, however, Julia has more in common with Eleanor Jaques than with Sonia, whom the publisher George Weidenfeld once cruelly described as a 'blowsy, reddish blonde'.

Julia is 'a bold-looking girl, of about twenty-seven with thick dark hair, a freckled face and swift, athletic movements'. That sounds much more like the dark-haired Eleanor than Sonia Brownell. Orwell's great friend Richard Rees defined Julia as 'intelligent but completely unintellectual', which again matches Eleanor Jaques far more than it does Sonia Brownell.

The scene in which she and Winston make love outdoors in the woods reprises that moment in 1932 when Orwell and Eleanor Jaques had sex in New Delight wood outside Walberswick. Orwell biographer Jeffrey Meyers calls it 'The most intensely erotic moment in Blair's life'. Bernard Crick believed it may have been 'his first serious *affaire*'.

Julia's body, we are told, 'gleamed white in the sun'. After sex, she falls asleep and Winston Smith pulls away her covering and 'studied her smooth white flank'. The language of *Nineteen Eighty-Four* at this point echoes Orwell's 1932 letter to Eleanor where he assures her he will 'always remember' the day they made love and her 'nice white body'.

That Orwell was thinking of Eleanor is suggested by another odd coincidence. When Orwell was living at 40 Stradbroke Road and Eleanor was at number 39, her next-door neighbour at number 37 was a Mr W. Smith.

'Winston Smith' was Orwell's version of himself, and 'Winston' is a sardonic tribute to Britain's wartime leader, who was the direct opposite of the thin, emaciated, weakling hero of *Nineteen Eighty-Four*. 'Smith' is one of the commonest British surnames and Orwell presumably used it to suggest that his hero is an Everyman figure – the common, ordinary man. But the Smiths were also once a prominent Southwold family and the churchyard of St Edmund's is packed with Smith graves. By yet another strange quirk of fate the candidate for the Independent Liberals who stood against the Tory candidate in Southwold in 1934 was one 'W. Smith'.

There were strong associations between the name 'Smith' and both Southwold and Eleanor Jaques, which were surely sloshing around in Orwell's subconscious while he was feverishly writing *Nineteen Eight-Four*.

I'm telling Paige all this as we walk on deeper into New Delight wood. We have the world to ourselves. No one else is out walking in this remote woodland on this crisp sunlit November day.

I suggest finding a suitable spot for our picnic. I point to where a narrow path leads off on the right, going deeper into the wood. Entering it, I realise no one has been this way for a while. The grass is untrodden and ferns crowd in, waist high. It's like wading across a green, gentle lake.

After ten minutes or so we come to a glade filled with sunlight. It's like a miniature amphitheatre – a circular depression surrounded on all sides by a high wall of ferns. We are in the heart of New Delight now, alone apart from the ring doves, which fill the wood with their soft coo-cooing.

I lay the groundsheet and the tartan rug on the ground and bring out the bottle of Sauvignon Blanc.

'Oh my God!' Paige cries. 'You actually brought wine glasses!'

I did, yes. I hate drinking good wine out of plastic cups.

I pour the wine.

'Cheers,' I say, and we clink glasses.

The wine is delicious, with a fresh, faintly lemony flavour. We sit cross-legged, in silence, drinking, listening to the cooing doves.

Paige finishes her glass and puts it down. Her expression is a strange mixture of the grave and the merry. It's as if she's finally decided the answer to a question and is pleasantly surprised. She looks at me with brazen eyes, tipping her head slightly back, which gives a faintly pugnacious thrust to her chin.

'Do you know how long it's been since I last had sex?' she says. 'Almost a year.'

'In my case,' I say, doing a quick calculation, 'about seven months.'

There's a moment in which we look at each other, half-smiling, a little wary.

'So we'd better not waste any more time,' I say, taking her hand.

'I guess not, mister,' she grins.

And then I'm unbuttoning her blouse and her hand drops and presses against me and soon we're naked and greedily kissing and stroking. And then we rock together, one flesh, our cries falling away into the trees, like birdsong.

Afterwards we lie in one another's arms, staring up at white fluffy clouds scudding by overhead like yachts in a race.

I start telling her about Veronica but she presses her finger against my lips and says: 'No autobiography.' Her finger runs down the inside of my thigh. She says: 'I don't want to know about you. And I don't want to tell you about me. This is just us, right? Here and now. Together for a little while.'

'Got it,' I reply, although I don't, not really.

Is she saying this is just a one-off? If so it's, well, *Orwellian*. His biography is littered with one-night stands.

I prop myself up on one elbow and gaze at her. Her breasts are plumper and more rounded than Ronnie's. Ronnie shaved herself completely, Paige has kept a carefully fashioned vertical strip of pubic hair.

Stop comparing them, I tell myself. *Forget Ronnie.*

Paige has a tattoo on the left cheek of her ass. A small blue butterfly. I reach for my phone. I want to take a photograph – an erotic souvenir – but she pushes me away, saying, 'No! Don't you dare! Ever!'

Her eyes flash. She looks angry. And then her eyes soften: 'Don't spoil it.'

'Sorry.'

And then she smiles. I'm forgiven. Her hand roams between my thighs and soon the glade is once again filled with our cries of pleasure.

Afterwards we dress and eat and finish the wine. Later we return down Lodge Lane in silence, hand in hand, with a blackbird singing its heart out by the bridge over the river.

'I'll be in touch,' she says, giving me one final kiss before she heads off along Pier Avenue.

10 There is a War

IT IS 5AM, THURSDAY May 20, 1937.

The bullet enters the neck just below the larynx, slightly at the left side of the vertical axis. It exits the body at the dorsal right side of the neck's base. The bullet is fired from a distance of approximately 175 yards. Upon impact it is travelling at a velocity of 600 feet per second. The bullet is a standard 7mm bore Spanish Mauser issue, plated with copper.

Orwell is catapulted backwards, on to his back.

No. Rewind.

Frank Frankford, another British volunteer, is standing beside Orwell at the moment the bullet hits. He catches him in his arms as Orwell topples.

No. Rewind.

Harry Milton, another British volunteer, is standing beside Orwell at the moment the bullet hits. He catches him in his arms as Orwell topples. 'When I put my hand under his neck there was a puddle of blood,' he remembered.

No. Rewind.

Nobody caught Orwell in their arms because it all happened so fast. He was on his back on the ground before anyone went to help.

Old men rewrite their past and they are always the heroes...

Orwell lies there, shot, bleeding.

Because the bullet has passed through the neck missing both the trachea and the carotid artery, Orwell will survive.

But Orwell is not fighting as George Orwell, writer. He signed up to fight in the Spanish Civil War as Eric Blair. Occupation: *grocer*.

Just after 2pm on Monday May 24, 1937 Southwold post

office receives a telegram for delivery to 36 High Street. It has been sent from Barcelona at noon. The telegraph boy with his peaked cap and smart uniform does not have far to walk to deliver it.

It reads ERIC SLIGHTLY WOUNDED PROGRESS EXCELLENT SENDS LOVE NO NEED FOR ANXIETY EILEEN.

The telegram downplays the initial seriousness of the situation. One of Orwell's vocal cords and his right arm are paralysed.

He is unable to speak.

I wake next morning to find a light coating of snow outside. Southwold is magical as more thick dense flakes blow in from the east. But by the afternoon the snow has turned to rain and the streets are dark and shining once again.

I sit close to the log burning stove, waiting for my phone to ring. I'm reading *Homage to Catalonia*. Arguably Orwell's second greatest book. As I plunge on through the vast forest of Orwell commentary I discover that *Homage to Catalonia* provoked two creative responses: one positive, one negative.

The film director Ken Loach produced his own homage in the form of the movie *Land and Freedom*. And the French novelist Claude Simon wrote a novel which mocks Orwell's book as a perversion of History.

I need to check them both out.

I've only seen one Ken Loach movie before. That was *The Wind That Shakes the Barley*. It had rave reviews and they were showing it as part of a retro season of past Cannes Film Festival winners. I took Ronnie to see it. After twenty minutes she walked out, whispering, 'If you want me I'll be in the bar.'

I stuck it out to the end.

Yeah, it was okay. But it didn't really move me and after all these years I don't really remember much about it, except that Cillian Murphy gets executed at the end. I remember much more afterwards finding Ronnie in the bar – this was a West End theatre, all red velvet and mirrors and plush cushioned seating. She was rocking with laughter at some joke the man she was next to had just told her. She'd laid her hand on his thigh and his forefinger was stroking the back of her hand. I walked up to her and said, 'Let's go.'

She looked at me and for a terrible moment I thought she was going to stay and go off into the night with her new friend. But she saw the cold look in my eyes and she knew me too well to play games.

She flung back her shoulders and angrily picked up her handbag and stalked off. Outside in the street we had a blazing row, then we went back to her apartment and had tremendous sex. For that, at least, thanks, Ken.

Land and Freedom. A dull title. It wouldn't have been out of place in the Soviet Union in the 1930s. And yes, I can see the *Homage to Barcelona* connection. Young unemployed man heads off to Spain, joins a P.O.U.M. militia group and discovers in the end that the Communists are intent on crushing the other revolutionary left groups, including his own. It's the tale of a revolution betrayed, much as Orwell's was.

But the plot has some key differences. The hero is a card-carrying member of the Communist Party, which Orwell never was. The militia group has attractive women fighting alongside the men and our hero duly falls in love with a black-haired Spanish beauty. She is killed and, although he gets back to England, marries and has children, we are led to believe she was the love of his life. *Land and Freedom* is told in flashbacks, as the hero's granddaughter goes through a suitcase of mementoes of his Spanish experience after his death.

When Paige phones two days later I invite her over to see it.

We watch it, side by side on the sofa, cradling our wine. Later Paige stretches out and lays her legs over mine. I gently, absently brush the inside of her thighs. She likes that. That's a turn-on.

And the action on the screen runs on.

At the end, as the credits roll, I see tears trickling down Paige's cheeks. 'That was so good,' she sighs. 'Didn't you think that was just *terrific*?'

'Not really,' I'm forced to confess.

Not really? She's aghast, wide-eyed, disbelieving. *Why not?*

I'll tell you why.

I mean, I can see it's a well-made movie. Top notch acting and all that. But it's not really a patch on Orwell's book. Orwell takes you on his own journey of understanding. He speaks directly to the reader in a clear, cogent voice. The story he has to tell is a complex one, crammed with detail.

Land and Freedom flattens everything out. It's a hollow film, where the sun never stops shining. Orwell was on the Aragon front in winter. It was cold and wet. It never rains once in *Land and Freedom*. Plus Loach doesn't make me care about any of the characters. They all seem cartoon-thin. Sorry, but I just don't think Ian Hart was right for the main role. He's a fine actor – I'm nagged by the knowledge I've seen him before and eventually I realise he was the private detective in the Ralph Fiennes/Julian Moore remake of *The End of the Affair* – but he's *not sexy*. I could see the romance coming a mile off and it struck me as a classic Hollywood device to engage the lazy viewer's interest.

I wasn't convinced that an ex-IRA man would choose to be buddies with an Englishman. I wasn't persuaded that after the Irishman is killed his incredibly stunning girlfriend would swiftly transfer her affections to the film's rather colourless protagonist.

Our hero is sincere but sincerity can quickly start to seem one-dimensional and dull. Sincerity is not one of the more gripping human emotions, dramatically speaking. And I wasn't entirely persuaded that there wouldn't have been resentment and jealousy among the Spaniards about their beautiful comrade fraternising first with an Irishman, then with an Englishman.

There are no women fighters in Orwell. On the contrary, he finds himself fighting alongside teenage boys. Orwell gives you the absurdity and unpleasant aspects of trench warfare. Comrades who shit in the trench. Hillsides coated in human excrement and the litter of thrown-away tin cans. Rain and mud and slime. Lice inside your clothes. There's a lot about lice in *Homage to Catalonia*. Itch, scratch, itch...

It never rains once in *Land and Freedom*. There's no litter, no excrement, no lice. Loach glorifies combat. The militia storm the Fascist lines while the Internationale plays stirringly on the soundtrack. *Land and Freedom* is an anti-Stalinist film which uses that most Stalinist of artistic forms, socialist realism. And socialist realism isn't *real*. It's bogus. Everybody's brave and comradely and, if anyone errs, they are instantly converted back to the one true cause.

'That's my take on the movie,' I conclude. 'Its heart is in the right place and its historical message is true. But it's not a great film. It just isn't.'

Paige shakes her head vehemently. Orwell writes women out of the struggle, she says. Ken Loach puts them back in.

We are never going to agree on this.

We finish the wine and make love on the carpet, warmed by the heat from the stove. Afterwards I walk her back to Pier Avenue. We pause outside her apartment and she sees the faint smile on my face.

'What are you thinking?'

'I'm thinking that if you invited me in I could stay all night and then we could get up just before dawn and take a walk along the beach and watch the sunrise. Maybe we could have sex in the dunes, before the first dog-walkers turn out.'

'You are a very naughty boy,' she laughs, her skin coppery-looking under the sodium street light. 'But I need my beauty sleep, as you Brits say. And I haven't finished the penultimate chapter yet. So, *no*.'

'Maybe just once. Some other night.'

'Don't count on it, mister.'

We exchange a quick kiss and after I've watched her go indoors and seen the lights go on upstairs I walk away.

I understand.

Modern woman needs her space.

Ken Loach romanticises and simplifies *Homage to Catalonia* but he stays true to its central message. The good guys – P.O.U.M. – were murderously repressed by the Communist Party. Stalin was a control freak and – historic irony – he hated the idea of revolution. Russia supplied the weaponry and called the shots. If the Spanish government wanted arms it had to suppress and lock up all the independent left groups – the Anarchists, the trade unionists, the Marxist splinter groups.

Orwell's experiences in Spain taught him that the Communist Party was a force for bad, not good. Communists locked up, tortured and murdered others on the left. The Soviet Union was a force for repression, not liberation. The Communist press told lie after lie after lie. The biggest lie of all was that the independent left groups in Spain were secretly colluding with Franco and the forces of fascism. What was even more obscene was that most of the left in Britain swallowed these lies.

Homage to Catalonia was intended to set the record straight about six months in one part of Spain during the civil war. And Orwell was right. He was a truth-teller. Modern historians do not seriously dispute his account or his interpretation. But Communist Party members and Stalin-worshippers never forgave Orwell for *Homage to Catalonia*. Which is where Claude Simon comes in.

I discover the connection via the book *Orwell's Victory*, by Christopher Hitchens. Claude Simon won the Nobel Prize for Literature in 1985, largely for his 1981 novel *Les Géorgiques* (translated into English by Beryl and John Fletcher and published by John Calder in 1989 as *The Georgics*). Hitchens notes Simon's grudge against Orwell, deplores the French writer's attempt to expose Orwell's supposedly bogus version of events in *Homage to Catalonia*, and concludes that 'The award of the Nobel Prize to such a shady literary enterprise is a minor scandal, reflecting the intellectual rot which had been spread by pseudo-intellectuals.'

Was Hitchens right?

I can't wait to find out.

I buy a second-hand copy of *The Georgics* from AbeBooks. It once belonged to Oak Park Public Library,

Oak Park, Illinois, where evidently there isn't much demand for experimental French fiction.

It's a novel in five parts, which moves from the French revolution to the twentieth century. Part Four is the one featuring a fictional Orwell. The dust jacket alludes to it, stating, 'We see a well-known English literary figure in the Spanish Civil War, and understand it through his eyes.'

A statement which, I discover, is a travesty. *The Georgics* does not seek to understand Spain through Orwell's eyes but rather to recycle selected episodes from *Homage to Catalonia* in a meretricious way. The intention is to denigrate Orwell. And it is telling that neither Claude Simon nor his publisher can quite bring themselves to use the words 'George Orwell'. Simon reduces him to a terse, one-letter abbreviation: 'O.' This is not accidental. *The Georgics* seeks to shrink Orwell and cut him down to size. He becomes a zero, a nothing.

Simon begins with Orwell on the run in Barcelona – in other words, he begins at the end of Orwell's involvement in Spain. But Orwell is not a heroic figure fleeing political repression. He is compared to a rat. He sinks 'into a kind of confused torpor'. Orwell, his wife and two companions manage to escape across the border into France. They get off at the first station, at 'a little fishing-town' where the waiters are hostile because the four travellers don't order from the expensive gourmet menu or leave huge tips. And already Claude Simon is perverting the historical record. He's a careless reader of *Homage to Catalonia* because, in fact, as Orwell makes clear, his two companions travelled on to Paris and only he and Eileen got off at the first station. And it is typical of Simon that he doesn't name the fishing town where Orwell and his wife stayed. That whole section of *The Georgics* which is devoted to denigrating Orwell is characterised by vagueness and imprecision – a massive irony when Simon's purpose is supposedly to set the record straight.

The town was called Banyuls. The reason why Orwell and his wife encountered hostility there was not because they were tight-fisted visitors who went for the cheapest dishes and were poor tippers but because, as Orwell explains in *Homage to Catalonia*, 'The little town seemed solidly pro-Franco.'

Another example of Simon's vicious truth-twisting occurs when he recycles the quip about how much easier it would be if the paving-stones of Barcelona were numbered, which would make it so much easier to build barricades and then put back the stones afterwards. Simon attributes the joke to 'one of the journalists – or double agents – staying in the hotel'. That's a characteristic slur. Orwell names the joker as 'George Tioli, an Italian journalist, a great friend of ours'. A double-agent? For which faction or country?

And so it goes on. Simon's purpose is plain. It is to show Orwell as a man hopelessly out of his depth, who understood nothing of what was going on around him. Orwell is identified as a man living in 'that kind of daze which will not cease growing, in which he still finds himself when, back in England, he begins writing the book in which he goes back over what he has experienced'. By a massive sleight of hand Claude Simon – vague, slippery, reducing everything to a meandering mush of manipulative prose – convicts George Orwell – precise in his names and dating, acknowledging his own partisan commitments – of being 'dreamy'.

Orwell begins *Homage to Catalonia* by describing his encounter with an Italian militiaman at the Lenin Barracks in Barcelona. It was a moment of solidarity between two foreigners who'd come to Spain to fight against Fascism. Orwell never forgot this momentary meeting with a fellow fighter whose handshake seemed to sum up the idealism and solidarity of the struggle. In 1942 Orwell wrote an essay, 'Looking Back on the Spanish War', which ended with verses written in memory of this militia man. It climaxed with the much-quoted lines:

But the thing that I saw in your face
No power can disinherit:
No bomb that ever burst
Shatters the crystal spirit.

And what response does the inspirer of this strangely tender and moving poetry evoke in Claude Simon? A sneer. A mean-spirited sarcasm.

Simon jeers that the militia man was an 'allegorical character'. He slyly suggests that the man never existed and that Orwell invented him. Then, having injected his venom, Simon seeks to draw some of it back, remarking with silky equivocation that the man is 'not entirely made up, exactly' but is merely a type. And, even though Orwell probably did meet someone who roughly resembled this fictitious or exaggerated militia man, he used the experience only in order 'to maintain his self esteem'. A few pages later Simon returns to the attack. With another sleight of hand he now refers to the Italian militia man as a 'mythical apparition'.

And so it goes on.

Claude Simon's entire narrative is a fraud. It purports to take us inside Orwell's mind but all the time it both falsifies Orwell's consciousness and frames it with the criticisms of a hostile and omniscient commentator. *Homage to Catalonia* is basically turned inside out by Claude Simon and made safe for Stalinist historiography. What Orwell witnessed with his own eyes in Catalonia was that the Communist Party was not interested in solidarity but control and that it was prepared to murder its political adversaries on the left on the most spurious of pretexts. Orwell himself narrowly escaped being imprisoned and quite possibly killed. With a contemptuous sneer Claude Simon states that 'from time to time he learned that one of his own sort, a Thompson or a Smillie, had been arrested'. Note that Claude Simon cannot bring himself to give these men their full names. He reduces them. He also turns them into objects – *things* – not people. And what happened to 'a Smillie'? Bob Smillie died in jail in Valencia in murky circumstances on June 13, 1937. He was probably beaten to death.

Perhaps the most astonishing indictment that Claude Simon levels against George Orwell is that in Catalonia he was 'blind and deaf to everything except what he perceived immediately around him'. A strange criticism to make of *Homage to Catalonia*, which is not a history treatise but rather an autobiographical account of one man's experiences. Claude Simon asserts that 'the bulk of his knowledge had been inculcated in him by books', which is a strange criticism to make of George Orwell, who did not go to university but rather to Burma, where he spent five years in exotic and violent outposts of the Empire. When he returned he went 'down and out' with tramps and then lived and worked among the desperate and the marginalised in Paris. Later he went hop-picking in Kent with East Enders. The very last person to have absorbed his knowledge of life from books was George Orwell.

It would be possible to write a book refuting Claude Simon's innumerable distortions of *Homage to Catalonia* but it just wouldn't be worth it. No one in Britain or the

USA reads Claude Simon anymore. He's a very, very minor French experimental writer. Where the *nouveau roman* is concerned it's Alain Robbe-Grillet who remains the focus of attention.

Claude Simon jeers at Orwell's style, referring to 'the romantic and dusty quality of the clichés with which he peppered his account' but people are still reading *Homage to Catalonia*. Its prose is fresh, vivid, visceral and quite the opposite of Claude Simon's, which is vague, slippery and seamed with equivocation. And dull.

So I'm with Hitchens on this.

Giving the Nobel Prize to Claude Simon for *The Georgics* was a disgrace.

Paige spends most of the week in Lowestoft, in the Records Office. She's consulting the Collings Collection – a substantial anthropological archive which once belonged to the Southwold Medical Officer, Dr Collings, and his son, Dennis. Dr Collings was a passionate Eygptologist, among many other things. His son, who married Eleanor Jaques, did a lot of anthropological work in Malaya (as it was then called) in the second half of the 1930s.

Paige reports back. No Orwell biographer has ever looked at this material before. And tucked away among the dry-as-dust scientific stuff is personal material. Including an old diary of Eleanor's, plus letters and postcards. It turns out that she was born in 1927 and came to Southwold when she was fourteen. Her family didn't live right next door to Orwell's family. They lived at number 39 Stradbroke Road, which isn't next door to number 40 but on the other side. It wasn't opposite, either, but some way down the road.

And guess who lived next door to Eleanor.

A Mr. W. Smith.

Whose first name, sadly, wasn't Winston.

Paige has also discovered a photograph of Dennis and Eleanor together with her family on the beach at Southwold. Even better, she's found a studio portrait of Eleanor as a teenager.

You know who that is, don't you?

That's *Nineteen Eighty-Four's* Julia.

Before she met Orwell.

11 Upset by Wisconsin

THERE'S A GIANT MOON AND I'm at the end of Southwold Pier with Paige, admiring it. The papers call it the Super Moon. There's a drift of thin cloud across it, obscuring the sharpness of the craters and dark plateaus.

'This is beautiful,' Paige says. She gestures at the band of moonlight cutting across the inky surface of the North Sea. The water rocks to and fro against the rusted pier supports like liquid silver.

'You sound sad,' I say. 'Why are you sad?'

'Do I? Perhaps it's because moonlight has that effect on me. There's something deathly about it.'

She hugs me, kisses me. We embrace, fiercely.

Then we hurry back to Vancouver Cottage.

Later, in bed, both of us drowsy with satisfied desire, I tell her about *The Georgics*.

'The guy is a complete shit,' I announce.

'Like Orwell, then,' says Paige.

Now, suddenly, she's back into critical mode. She jerks fully awake. She's not defending Claude Simon, who she's not read. She's telling me about Orwell's blindness to women. His notions of masculinity. 'You know why he liked Spain so much? He was in a world of men. The boys of the militia literally looked up to him. *Homage to Catalonia* is a rhapsody to masculinity.'

'That's not fair,' I protest. 'There were women who fought in Spain. It wasn't Orwell's fault he blundered into a situation where he served in a militia group that was all male.'

Paige snorts. 'And didn't he love it! No annoying vegetarians or sandal wearers. No *pansy poets*. No birth control advocates. Just good clean fighting men embracing war. And you know the end of that book? That stuff about England being asleep and that the roar of bombs is coming to wake everybody up? There's an undertone of joy about it. He's secretly embracing it. He wants to see war and destruction. And you know why? Because it will toughen up a nation gone soft. It will turn boys into men. Real men, who shoot guns.'

'You're seeing things that aren't there,' I hotly retort.

'I'm not. They're there. It's just a question of point of view.'

I fall silent. 'Let's talk about this tomorrow,' I say.

'Coward.'

'That's me. Unmanly.'

Paige reaches down under the sheet and I feel the movement of her hand.

'I wouldn't say that,' she says, smiling.

The smile of an imp.

A mischief maker.

One Orwell book leads to another Orwell book.

It's a maze which promises a final understanding.

But each turn of the maze leads to another turn. The centre is never reached.

Or rather, there is no shortage of people who claim to have got there. Problem is, they are all standing in different places.

All the biographies list one of the earliest books every published on him: *A Study of George Orwell* by Christopher Hollis. I snap up a second-hand copy. It's less than a fiver – very cheap for a first edition with a clean dust jacket. The book was published in 1956. Its pitch is simple. This is the first book to offer inside information about George Orwell's life. Its subtitle is *The Man and his Works*.

Orwell had been dead for six years but very little was known about his life. Hollis boasted of his special knowledge of the man:

> Mr Christopher Hollis knew George Orwell, or Eric Blair as he was really called, during his schooldays at Eton, afterwards in Burma and at the end of his life. His study of Orwell's books is therefore illuminated by some anecdotes of reminiscence.

This is classic PR spin. Hollis barely knew Orwell at all. At Eton, Hollis, who was older, was in a different year. Years later he happened to bump into Orwell once in Burma when he was passing through. They had a meal and a chat. End of.

Orwell was a quiet networker and he kept in touch with a huge range of people, including Hollis. But Hollis, who was a devout Catholic and became a Conservative MP, was never close to Orwell. He didn't think Eric Blair was particularly interesting and he didn't keep a letter he once received from him.

Hollis was floundering in the dark. Orwell's letter was sent from Southwold but because Hollis threw it away he couldn't quite remember where he was living. Hollis describes it as *a little village on the River Orwell*. Nice try. But Southwold is on the coast, not on a river. And although there is a river nearby it is the Blyth, not the Orwell. It's a myth that Orwell had anything to do with the river which bears that name. At best he saw it in the distance from the window of a train coming into Ipswich. There were no personal connections at all.

Geography wasn't Hollis's strong point. He states that 'By 1936 Orwell's circumstances were a little easier and he was able to move out of London, which he detested, into

Essex, where he kept a village store.'

Essex?

Hollis is alluding to 2 Kits Lane, Wallington, Hertfordshire. And it's by no means the only blunder. Hollis states that 'He went to Spain, financed by an advance from Secker and Warburg for the writing of his reminiscences.' Complete garbage. Orwell had no connection at all with Secker and Warburg at that point in his life. At the time he went to Spain he was desperately short of money. He financed his own trip.

Christopher Hollis, MP, is also curiously priggish when it comes to sex. Orwell's enthusiasm for Henry Miller makes him wince. 'The *Tropic of Cancer*, when all is said and done,' he pompously asserts, 'is a pathetic business of James Joyce for Wisconsin sophomores.'

So, not a Joyce fan either. And what did Wisconsin ever do to upset uptight, sniffy Christopher Hollis?

Plus someone who believes that Henry Miller and James Joyce are similar writers plainly doesn't grasp that their differences as literary authors are far greater than any superficial similarities in their treatment of sex.

But let's not be too hard on Hollis. If his claim to have special knowledge of Orwell by virtue of a long acquaintance was a wild exaggeration, his book is not without interest. Bizarrely, it's an attempt to reclaim Orwell for Christianity. And although the premise is fundamentally absurd, Hollis's identification of a deeply conservative aspect to Orwell's intellectual make-up is perfectly plausible.

After all, Orwell requested in his will that he should be buried according to the rites of the Church of England.

He ended up being interred alongside a former British prime minister. *Historic irony.*

12 So-shall-ism

'ORWELL'S SOCIALISM IS A BATTLEGROUND, best avoided by those who do not wish to find themselves in a slough of hot-tempered tedium,' quips John Sutherland, deftly extracting all the teeth from the mouth of an energetic chewer-over of the politics of everything.

Englishness, democracy, fascism, freedom, and all that jive.

I doubt if Orwell would have agreed with Professor Sutherland. After all, he wrote:

> The impulse of every writer is to 'keep out of politics'. What he wants is to be left alone so that he can go on writing books in peace. But unfortunately it is becoming obvious that this ideal is no more practicable than that of the petty shopkeeper who hopes to preserve his independence in the teeth of the chain-stores.

He wrote that in June 1938 in his essay 'Why I Joined the Independent Labour Party'.

It makes me think of a sentiment attributed to Trotsky. I say attributed because a lefty friend once quoted it at me but I have no source for it and it may be apocryphal, like Lenin and useful idiots. What Trotsky is reputed to have said is: 'You may not care about foreign policy but foreign policy cares about you.'

Paige leans over my shoulder and looks at my laptop screen. I feel her warmth. She smells of a creamy fragrance. She reads what I've just typed.

'So, to Orwell all writers were automatically presumed to be *men*,' she hisses. 'It's all about what *he* wants.'

Go away, Paige. We'll argue about Orwell and feminism

in another chapter.

Paige turns. She recedes.

I can hear her washing up, clattering dishes. A feminist in the kitchen, tidying up after her man. She needs to watch out. She's in danger of turning into Eileen O'Shaughnessy.

Conservatives see the man who in *Nineteen Eighty-Four* showed the horrors which result from socialism and who in *Animal Farm* showed how revolution always ends in tyranny.

I buy an old second-hand copy of *Nineteen Eighty-Four* and inside it someone has sellotaped a newspaper cutting dated 10 October 1980. The sticky tape and the cutting have both turned yellow and I struggle to read the tiny font. In the end I manage to decipher it. It's from the Conservative Party Conference of October 1980. It reads:

In conclusion Mrs Thatcher said: 'Let Labour's Orwellian nightmare of the Left be the spur for us to dedicate with a new urgency our every ounce of energy and moral strength to rebuild the fortunes of this free nation.'

Wild cheering and a standing ovation, I expect...

A travesty!

Socialists retort that Orwell was quite explicit about where he stood. 'My recent novel is NOT intended as an attack on Socialism or on the British Labour Party (of which I am a supporter).' He wrote that on 16 June 1949.

Spain was the turning point.

On 8 June 1937 he wrote to his friend Cyril Connolly: 'I have seen wonderful things and at last really believe in Socialism which I never did before.'

*

A muggy December day.

The sea seems thick as oil. Its unrippled surface stretches out under a plum-coloured sky which seems heavy with the possibility of a storm. It's the quietist I've seen it. It's low tide and at ten in the morning the beach is deserted.

At the end, where the river empties into the North Sea, a pair of turnstones scamper across the weed-strewn sand. They rush across the beach, then halt and peck furiously. Then they run on. They are curiously tame, not bothered by my presence at all.

At the harbour, on the far side, where the old harbour wall is ragged with decay, two cormorants are drying their wings.

I'm listening to Lana del Rey. Her duet with Julian Lennon blows me away.

I like heartbreak songs best.

The band is playing an old Glenn Miller number. A jazzy wartime song, 'Under The Spreading Chestnut Tree'.

It's on YouTube. It's dated but I like it. A jaunty, upbeat little number. And, yes – Orwell probably did have this old Glenn Miller song in mind when he used his own bitter, twisted version of a song with the same name in *Nineteen Eighty-Four*.

But now, at the back of the bar, there's a fight going on. It's the left, falling out among themselves again.

I think I recognise that guy with the sexy stubble, the slightly plump face. He's taking a swing at everyone who gets near him. Someone has told him to put his cigarette out but he's shouting that this is America, land of the free! He's a bit drunk, that's obvious.

It's the Hitch!

AKA the late Christopher Hitchens.

But who else has come to the party?

More ghosts. All the crackling voices of the dead.

Spectres are haunting Orwell – the spectres of his Left critics.

Isaac Deutscher was the first one to arrive, back in 1954. He didn't like *Nineteen Eight-Four*. He thought it was the work of a 'fear-ridden and restricted imagination'.

There was nothing in the novel for progressives. The book was 'a document of dark disillusionment not only with Stalinism but with every form and shade of socialism'. The origins of Orwell's malaise lay not simply in Stalin's repression but in a broader difficulty: 'Like most British socialists, Orwell had never been a Marxist.' And so it was that 'grappling with the Purges, his mind became infected by their irrationality'.

Deutscher believed that Orwell at the end of his life reduced all politics to a single motive: the sadistic hunger for power. In *Nineteen Eighty-Four* the party of Big Brother has no political programme. Poverty and inequality exist purely to satisfy a pleasure in sadism. The Inner Party has no social purpose: 'It is a phantom-like emanation of all that is foul in human nature.'

Nineteen Eighty-Four was Stalinist terror transplanted to London. It was where 'Ingsoc' – English socialism – was heading. The novel was cold war propaganda which simplified the complexity of social change, politics and international relations. Orwell's novel 'has taught millions to look at the conflict between East and West in terms of black and white, and it has shown them a monster bogy and a monster scapegoat for all the ills that plague mankind'.

But Deutscher's critique had little impact. It was buried away in a volume of essays for an academic audience.

It took two decades before an assault on Orwell's politics reached a wide audience.

Raymond Williams, a prominent literary intellectual of the fifties, sixties and seventies, piled in with *Orwell* (1971). This was a slim monograph in a glossy paperback series pitched at undergraduates ('Fontana Modern Masters' – a title indicating that feminism had yet to reach the world of British publishing).

Williams diagnosed a number of ailments in the Orwell body politic. Firstly, Orwell had never really perceived capitalism as an economic and political system. Instead of a class-based analysis in which there was a war between 'the owners of property and capital and the owners only of labour and skill', Orwell falls back on the homely metaphor of England as 'a family with the wrong members in control'. The metaphor is flawed at every level. It's a simplistic and sentimental view of society and there's no sense of family in the depressed and suffering England of *The Road to Wigan Pier*. And Orwell's cosy image focuses on aunts and uncles. Above all it excludes the figure of *the father*.

Orwell resists and excludes the reality of working-class political organisation, always substituting individual experience. In the Midlands he met working-class socialists and members of the Unemployed Workers' Movement. This contact enabled him to go down a mine, and it was from these socialist activists that he obtained facts about housing conditions. But the experience of militant working-class social and political networks, which is set out in his diary, was omitted from *The Road to Wigan Pier*.

The roots of *Animal Farm* and *Nineteen Eighty-Four* are found in this earlier text: 'both the consciousness of the workers and the possibility of authentic revolution are denied'. He cuts out the spring of hope, says Williams. He projects an immense apathy on *all* the oppressed:

> By viewing the struggle as one between only a few people over the heads of an apathetic mass, Orwell created the conditions for defeat and despair.

But the Orwellian rot set in long before *Nineteen Eighty-Four*. That's what another prominent cultural figure of the 1960s and 1970s argued.

Enter the socialist historian, E. P. Thompson, best known for his classic book *The Making of the English Working Class*.

'Inside *Which* Whale?' he asked in an essay published in 1960, alluding to Orwell's long essay 'Inside the Whale', published exactly twenty years earlier, at the start of the Second World War.

In 'Inside the Whale' Orwell looked back over the thirties and concluded: 'Progress and reaction have both turned out to be swindles.' Thompson zooms in through the beady eye of a historian: '"Swindle" is an imprecise tool of analysis, a noise of disgust'.

He accuses Orwell of the wholesale and indiscriminate rejection of an entire socialist culture.

> He is sensitive – sometimes obsessionally so – to the least insincerity upon his left, but the inhumanity of the right rarely provoked him to a paragraph of polemic. To the right ('decent people,' 'average thinking person'), every allowance; to the left ('bearded fruit-juice drinkers who come flocking towards the smell of "progress" like bluebottles to a dead cat'), no quarter. What is noticeable about Orwell's characterisation of Communism in *Inside the Whale* is that time after time his prejudices are angry,

antagonistic responses to the ruling left orthodoxy, so laying the basis for a new orthodoxy-by-opposition.

Yes, it's true. Orwell, who had *a very weird moustache*, had a bit of a thing about men with beards. Odd.

Orwell also had a strange, violent antipathy to fruit juice.

And vegetarians.

And sandals.

But Edward Thompson is cheating a little. His 'bearded fruit-juice drinkers' quote doesn't come from 'Inside the Whale' (as anyone who didn't know their Orwell might think) but from the notorious second half of *The Road to Wigan Pier*.

Thompson adds:

We should also note another characteristic device of Orwell's polemic. He continually replaced the examination of objective situations by the imputation of motive.

Socialist idealism was not only discounted, it was also *explained away* as the function of middle-class guilt, frustration or ennui.

'Inside the Whale', Thompson argued, falsified the historical record of socialist activism in the 1930s. It mocked the idea of unselfish dedication to a political cause. Its pessimism about socialist activism in the end only served the interests of reaction. 'Inside the Whale' was an apology for quietism. 'It was in this essay, more than any other, that the aspirations of a generation were buried... But it is not the epitaph which the historical thirties deserved.'

After reading Thompson's hatchet job I read 'Inside the

Whale' for the first time. And I'm surprised to find it's nothing like I was expecting. The essay is basically an idiosyncratic account of English fiction and poetry in the inter-war years, framed by a critical analysis of two novels by Henry Miller.

When Orwell published his essay in 1940, Miller was a writer whose work was banned in Britain on the grounds of obscenity. The two writers had met in Paris in 1936. Orwell was on his way to participate in the Spanish civil war. Miller told him he couldn't understand why. Henry Miller had no interest in politics. As a writer he preferred to stay 'inside the whale' – in other words, inside his own little world, which moved with the tides. Orwell pursued the metaphor in an analysis of writers and their politics. 'Between 1935 and 1939 the Communist Party had an almost irresistible fascination for any writer under forty.'

Now I can see there are things to object to in Orwell's account of the period. His hypocrisy can at times be spectacularly breathtaking. He says that about 1928 *Punch* magazine published a very funny cartoon about 'an intolerable youth' who announced that he intended to 'write'. When asked what he was going to write about, the youth blandly replied: 'one doesn't write *about* anything, one just *writes*'. But that was *exactly* Eric Arthur Blair's situation in 1928. He was determined to be a writer but he didn't have a clue what sort of writer. A poet? A novelist? A reviewer? A literary critic? A biographer? A short-story writer? A journalist? A translator? The young Blair blundered and blathered, trying all sorts. But all the time he *wrote*. And it took him five years of serious dedication before he came up with a manuscript that was worth publishing.

When he says that the literary history of the 1930s

justifies the opinion that a writer does well to keep out of politics, it's a gross exaggeration. His own *Homage to Catalonia* originates in Orwell himself being swept up by the mood of the time. W. H. Auden's poetry of that decade isn't exactly second rate. And Orwell could sometimes be a lazy and careless polemicist. He rages against Auden's poem, 'You're leaving now, and it's up to you boys', calling it 'priggish' and 'pure scout-master'.

In fact the poem wasn't by Auden at all. It was the first line of a poem in *The Magnetic Mountain* by the wooden and now unread poet Cecil Day-Lewis.

Orwell had a weakness for windy, dogmatic generalisation. 'No decade in the past hundred and fifty years has been so barren of imaginative prose as the nineteen-thirties,' he thundered.

Oh yeah?

This was the decade of Aldous Huxley's *Brave New World* and Virginia Woolf's *The Waves* and Evelyn Waugh's *A Handful of Dust* and Malcolm Lowry's *Ultramarine* and Stella Gibbons's *Cold Comfort Farm* and Winifred Holtby's *South Riding* and Daphne du Maurier's *Rebecca* and Edward Upward's *Journey to the Border* and Christopher Isherwood's *Goodbye to Berlin* and Graham Greene's *The Confidential Agent* and Elizabeth Bowen's *The Death of the Heart* and Patrick Hamilton's *Twenty Thousand Streets Under the Sky*. Not such a bad collection of richly diverse fiction, was it?

'It was a time of labels, slogans, and evasions,' he boomed.

Which is the kind of vague label you could attach to any decade of the past century.

Everything is thunder without illumination.

What precisely was 'the political racket'? *Which*

'propaganda campaigns' and 'squalid controversies'?

There's no detail. Nothing to investigate.

But the same applies to E. P. Thompson's retort.

Both polemicists are hurling big blocks of rhetoric but the surfaces are smooth, shiny and impenetrable.

In 1984 there was (inevitably) a rash of books published about Orwell. Some were reminiscences by people who'd known him. Others were academic studies. Some were political critiques.

On the politics front fighting broke out again, big time.

Former war correspondent and foreign correspondent Alaric Jacob didn't pull his knuckleduster-coated punches.

For me *Nineteen Eighty-Four* is one of the most disgusting books ever written – a book smelling of fear, hatred, lies and self-disgust by comparison with which the works of the Marquis de Sade are no more than the bad dreams of a sick man

Crikey! A bit OTT, eh?

Robert Stradling, of University College, Cardiff, laid into *Homage to Catalonia*. 'The evidence,' he complained, 'strongly suggests that Orwell did no background reading on matters Iberian before he went to Spain'.

That's right – Orwell just turned up for the fight against fascism and then reported on his experiences. It was shockingly irresponsible of him not to have first read Professor Smudge's *Agrarian Economic Development in North East Spain* and Dr Karp's *Maritime Trade in Catalonia 1850-1930* before he went.

Stradling charmingly suggests that Orwell was a liar. Orwell famously criticised W. H. Auden for the line 'The

conscious acceptance of guilt in the necessary murder',
arguing that such a line was too easy and cheap and could
have been written only by someone with no personal
experience of murder. He himself, Orwell wrote, had
witnessed the aftermath of murder: 'the howling relatives...
the blood, the smells'. Murder was a terrible thing. It ought
not to be celebrated or regarded as a regrettable necessity.

Cardiff's Stradling pounces. *What murder victims?*
There is no evidence at all that Orwell witnessed any such
sights in Spain, therefore 'that he invented this story to gain
a moral advantage over the hapless Auden, although even
more damaging to Orwell's reputation, seems nevertheless
the more likely'.

Except that Orwell nowhere claimed to have witnessed
murders in Spain. His reputation emerges unscathed from
Stradling's critique. The allusion was to his days as a
colonial policeman in Burma between 1922 and 1927. It was
a very violent country, where gang murders were
commonplace. Orwell knew what he was talking about and
he was criticising Auden from the perspective of personal
experience.

Plus, Auden later changed that particular line of the
poem.

That's telling.

It suggests that the poet accepted the truth of Orwell's
scorching criticism.

13 Hand Grenades and Poltergeists

THE SUMMER OF 1940.

There was a war going on.

But you'd hardly notice.

On the train between Guildford railway station and Waterloo a traveller noticed *all along the line young men in flannels were playing cricket in the sunshine on beautifully tended fields shaded by stalwart oaks and poplar trees.* A little known Frenchman named General de Gaulle rocked up in London on 9 June and noticed that the city and its inhabitants had *a look of tranquillity, almost of indifference. The streets and parks full of people peacefully out for a walk, the long queues at the entrances to cinemas...* To de Gaulle it all *belonged to another world than the one at war.*

But not everyone was sunk in apathy or escapism. Three days earlier George Orwell wrote in his diary: *Everything is disintegrating. It makes me writhe to be writing book reviews etc. at such a time, and even angers me that such time wasting should be permitted.*

The last British troops left Dunkirk on 4 June. The headline in the *Daily Mirror* said it was BLOODY MARVELLOUS. Winston Churchill was less upbeat. He described it as a 'colossal military disaster', adding: 'Wars are not won by evacuations.'

It was widely assumed that the German military's next move would be an invasion of England. Orwell believed it too. He was worried that the civilian population was unprepared for this eventuality. He wrote an anxious letter to *Time and Tide*, making some helpful suggestions.

Sir: It is almost certain that England will be invaded within the next few days or weeks, and a large-scale invasion by sea-borne troops is quite likely. At such a time our slogan should be ARM THE PEOPLE. [...]

ARM THE PEOPLE is in itself a vague phrase, and I do not, of course, know what weapons are available for immediate distribution. But there are at any rate several things that can and should be done *now*, i.e. within the next three days:

1. Hand grenades. [...] They are said to be useful against tanks and will be absolutely necessary if enemy parachutists with machine-guns manage to establish themselves in our big towns. [...] armed men can be driven out of stone buildings with grenades if the right tactics are used.

2. Shotguns. [...] many gunsmiths' windows show rows of guns which are not only useless where they are, but actually a danger, as these shops could easily be raided. The powers and limitations of the shotgun [...] should be explained to the public over the radio.

3. Blocking fields against aircraft landings. [...] In a small thickly-populated country like England we could within a very few days make it impossible for an aeroplane to land anywhere except at an aerodrome. [...]

4. Painting out place-names. This has been well done as regards sign-posts, but there are everywhere shopfronts, tradesmen's vans, etc., bearing the name of their locality. Local authorities should have the power to enforce the painting-out of these immediately. [...]

5. Radio sets. Every Local Defence Volunteer headquarters should be in possession of a radio receiving set [...] It is fatal to reply on the telephone in a moment of emergency. [...]

All of these are things which could be done within the space of a very few days. Meanwhile, let us go on repeating ARM THE PEOPLE, in the hope that more and more voices will take it up.

'Orwell the urban guerrilla,' I say to Paige. '*Cool.*'
She shrugs.
She yawns.
She goes on reading her book. Her face like a bronze mask. California skin – healthy, sun-lashed, embodying all the merits of regular exercise, a diet rich in vitamins and lots of satisfying sex.
Her book. Light reading. A slim paperback.
Marguerite Duras, *The Lover.*
Published in – wait for it – 1984.

Orwell in the summer of 1940 was in a state of frenzied revolutionary euphoria. He was convinced that Britain's reactionary ruling class would sell out to Hitler and negotiate a grovelling Vichy-style compromise. All that stood in the way was an insurrection by the working class. He followed up his call to arms with a long pamphlet, *The Lion and the Unicorn.* Public schools must be suppressed! Incomes must be levelled out, to get rid of the rich! Land, banks and major industries must be nationalised! India must be given independence! Either that, or lose the war!

But the ruling class did not capitulate to the Fuehrer. Even the reactionaries rallied round. Nationalism proved superior to Hitler-worship. And the working class showed no impulse to rise up against its masters.

Peter Sedgwick: "From this point on, Orwell's explicit politics become vaguer. For him, politics was always excessively 'the art of the possible' and once it became evident that the British ruling class could wage an anti-Fascist war, and that the working class were not ready for insurrection, he ceased to advocate revolution."

And although he was writhing and angry at the futility of it all, and boiling with ideas about arming the workers, Orwell continued writing book reviews.

That same month, June 1941, he reviewed Jim Phelan's book *Jail Journey*, about the author's life as a long-term prisoner. Orwell was enthusiastic: 'In a book that is always lively and readable, the thing that stands out as truly important is Mr. Phelan's straightforward discussion of the sex life of prisons.' Masturbation, buggery, homosexuality: 'Over sixty unnatural forms of the sexual act, he says, are now practised in Dartmoor and Parkhurst.' Orwell also found 'very interesting if true' Phelan's claim that the majority of women go in for some form of exhibitionism when they pass a file of convicts on the road.

'Women flashing at men in chains,' I tell Paige. 'Kinky.'

'I don't believe a word of it,' she says. 'This guy Phelan was a fantasist.'

'Orwell believed him.'

'Orwell wanted to. You can see the idea excited him. At heart he was just a dirty little boy.'

'Unfair. And no one's ever said that before.'

'Yeah, well, look at the Orwell bibliographers, buster. Book after book. All written by men. A species with deformed optics.'

'Unfair.'

'It's okay. I've learned to compensate. Even if they haven't.'

*

139

That sultry summer another book rolled in for Orwell to review.

Poltergeists.

Subtitle: *An Introduction and Examination followed by Chosen Instances.* By Sacheverell Sitwell, with decorations by Irene Hawkins and silhouettes by Cruikshank. First published in June 1940 by Faber and Faber Limited, 24 Russell Square, London W. C. 1.

Orwell loved it.

So much so that he wrote a fan letter to the author.

6 July 1940
18 Dorset Chambers
Chagford Street
Ivor Place NW 1

Dear Mr Sitwell,

I had your book on poltergeists to review for "Horizon" and was very interested by it. I could only do a review of about 600 words and I don't know whether they'll print all of that, as they haven't much space. When I read that very creepy incident you describe of the girl medium dressing dummies or arranging clothes about the room, it brought back to me a memory of 10 years ago which I thought you might like to hear, as I believe it has a remote bearing on your subject.

Flashback to 1930.

Orwell had returned to Southwold, living once more with his mother, father and younger sister. He wouldn't meet his future wife Eileen for another five years. His life wasn't going well. It was now three years since he'd grandly announced to the parentals that he was chucking in his well-paid job as a colonial policeman in order to become a writer. What had he got to show for it? Zilch. Well, not quite zilch. One or two poems, in a world burdened with mountains of bad or merely competent verse. Some reviews in little magazines. Nothing to boast about.

He'd gone off to Paris, city of James Joyce, Hemingway and F. Scott Fitzgerald. But he hadn't mingled with the literary set (although he thought he might once have spotted Joyce in the distance). In Paris he wrote two novels, evidently at high-speed, turbo-charged with creative enthusiasm and ambition. They were both rejected. In despair he destroyed them. He poured out short stories. But he couldn't get even a short story accepted.

Now he was back home. A failure. He was coming up to his twenty-seventh birthday. Just another failed wannabe writer. Plus he didn't even have a girlfriend. How sad is that?

Plus his savings had run out.

He had to find work.

Which is how Orwell came to be hanging out in Walberswick.

He was employed to tutor Bryan Morgan, a physically disabled boy with learning difficulties, whose parents lived in Walberswick, the village on the other side of the river to Southwold.

Nowadays Walberswick is even more exclusive than Southwold.

Southwold could boast second homes owned by the novelist Julie Myerson and the crime writer, P.D. James. (Oddly P.D. James owned 1 Queen Street, right next door to 3 Queen Street, where Orwell was living in 1930.)

But Walberswick can currently boast five resident celebrities: the film director Richard Curtis, plus his wife Emma Freud, plus Emma's novelist sister Esther Freud, who is married to the actor David Morrissey. Not to mention the film director Paul Greengrass, who has long dreamed of a remake of *Nineteen Eighty-Four*.

I've wandered over to Walberswick quite a few times since I first came to Vancouver Cottage and I've never seen any of them. Even though it's out of season and peak celebrity-spotting season.

The other day someone tweeted that they'd seen Johnny Depp in Southwold. He was in the High Street and he patted someone's dog. A lovely man.

I'll believe that when I see Johnny myself.

In 1930 Walberswick was nowheresville. A dull little village which had been in decline ever since the Suffolk sheep trade collapsed at the end of the Middle Ages.

To reach Walberswick and his new paid employment, Orwell stepped out of the imposing front entrance of number 3 and turned right down Queen Street. He passed the Red Lion and cut across South Green to the footpath which ran across the marshes behind the houses on Ferry Road. At the start of the path, on the left, was the old abandoned salt works building, a fragment of which is still there today.

A brisk ten minutes' walk.

At the end the path rose up to meet Blackshore and the ferry ramp. The ferry was a steam pontoon named after the river which it crossed. *The Blyth* moved to and fro on a fixed route between two chains, powered by a 'donkey' boiler. It carried up to twenty passengers and goods or vehicles weighing up to two tons. In 1930 the ferry made over 25,000 crossings of this short stretch of muddy brown river.

Tutor to Bryan Morgan...

What did that involve?

Apparently, keeping the lad occupied. Superior child-minding. Bryan had suffered from polio. He had difficulty using his hands but he was able to walk, so Orwell took him on excursions around the village.

One day they were on Walberswick Common when the boy spotted a neatly tied parcel under a gorse bush. Inside was a cardboard box about the size of a small shoebox. The box was lined with cloth and contained a miniature room with model furniture and women's clothes in miniature, including underwear. There was also a note addressed to the person opening the parcel: *This is not bad is it?*

WTF?

This was *seriously weird*. It was straight out of a Sherlock Holmes story. *The curious case of the Walberswick miniaturist.*

Orwell believed that only a woman could have been responsible for this enigmatic and delicately constructed model. It obviously wasn't Bryan Morgan, because the polio had made him clumsy with his hands. Whoever had made the model had gone to a lot of time and effort. But why then hide it in such a remote location?

Orwell was certain that it had been put there with the deliberate intention of someone finding it. That person, he believed, must be a local woman – a resident of Walberswick. But she must also be *suffering from some kind of sexual aberration.*

If he was still a cop Orwell was confident he could, after making enquiries, identify the suspect. But no crime had been committed and he was no longer a cop. Orwell wrapped up the box again and put it back where they'd found it. When he and Bryan returned a few days later the package had gone.

*

'I see,' says Paige. 'Another kinky woman. Orwell really had a thing about the species, didn't he?'

'He was just reporting an experience.'

'Yeah, right... One old Etonian to another.'

'Eh?'

'Oh, didn't you know? Sitwell was educated at Eton.' The smile on her face deepens. 'Small world, eh, buster?' She adds with a snort: '*Limeys.*'

We chill.

We watch *From Here to Eternity.*

Frank Sinatra is a whole lot better than I ever imagined he could be as an actor.

Later, in bed, she says: 'Nobody ever kissed me the way you do.'

We are all postmodernists now.

Orwell described that strange experience on Walberswick Common in his letter to Sacheverell Sitwell. He wrote:

> I have often puzzled over the incident since, and always with the feeling that there was something vaguely unwholesome in the appearance of the little room and the clothes. Then in your book you linked up the doll-dressing impulse in girls with definite mental aberration, and it struck me that this affair had a sort of bearing on the subject. The fact that I promptly remembered the incident when reading that passage in your book seems to establish a kind of connection.

Reading that I know I have to get hold of a copy of *Poltergeists.*

This is easily accomplished. There are a number of second-hand copies for sale on internet sites, so I order one.

It doesn't have the original dust jacket but then I'm acquiring it as a reader, not a book collector who wants to prize it as a rare object. I splash out on expedited delivery and it arrives the next day. This is the wonder of twenty-first century life. In the last century I could have spent years browsing in second-hand bookshops before I finally found a copy.

The episode which fascinated Orwell turns out to be in Sitwell's long (seventy-five pages!) Introduction.

It's identified as 'The curious Phelps case' and it occurred in the village of Stratford, Connecticut, in the period 1850-1851. The events happened inside the home of the Reverend Doctor Eliakim Phelps, a Presbyterian minister.

Phelps treated diseases using mesmerism. He also believed in spiritualism and clairvoyance. He married 'late in life' (how late?) a widow with four children: two girls, aged sixteen and six, and two boys, aged eleven and three. In March 1850 Phelps contacted

a gentleman from New York, who came to him, at Stratford, in order that they should hold séances and try to obtain replies, through rapping, to questions that they asked. These attempts were, apparently, successful.

A few days later, on 10 March 1850, the minister returned home from church. He found the house in chaos. Furniture had been tipped over in every room. It was as if burglars had broken in and ransacked the property. But nothing was missing.

Something even more bizarre and sinister had occurred. In one room eleven figures had been created, dressed in clothes, forming a strange tableau – the representation of a group of people at prayer. Ten were female. The figures were arranged in postures of extreme devotion. Some were bent forwards with their foreheads almost touching the floor. Others knelt with open Bibles in front of them. The pages were open at passages which were regarded as highly significant to the tableau. In the middle was the figure of a dwarf, grotesquely dressed. Above the dwarf was a figure suspended, as if flying through the air.

Kinda weird, huh?

The disturbances continued for eighteen months. Furniture continued to be toppled. Household objects were thrown about. Windowpanes were broken. Mysterious written messages appeared on the walls. There was persistent rapping. When interrogated, the raps responded with blasphemous replies.

The oldest boy's clothes were cut to ribbons.

On a later occasion the boy was found hung to a tree, and the elder girl, while sleeping, had a pillow pressed over her head and tape tied round her neck, which almost strangled her...

And the sinister puppet figures continued to be constructed and set up in tableau arrangements.

Once, outside the eldest girl's bedroom, loud raps were heard from within, followed by the sound of the girl crying out in shock. The girl had a deep red mark on her face, where, she said, she had been struck by an invisible hand.

The disturbances lasted from 10 March 1850, to 1 October 1851.

Sacheverell Sitwell concluded that the three primary instigators of these mysterious events were the mother, Mrs Phelps, and her two eldest children. The assaults on the two children were surely 'trickery and imposture' and, he believed, carried out by the children themselves. The daughter had 'turned diabolist' and manufactured the weird praying figures.

But if the poltergeist phenomenon could be explained away as being the work of human and not paranormal agencies, did that really *explain* what it was all about? Sacheverell Sitwell:

> And should all this trickery be unmasked as the work of Harry and his sister of sixteen, does it, we may ask, make the mystery less mysterious? Not so phenomenal, but just as unpleasant, and just as difficult to explain.

George Orwell, like Sitwell, was a sceptic. In his review for *Horizon* he asserted that 'Ghosts are completely uninteresting, but the aberrations of the human mind are not.' In the case of the poltergeist activity in the Phelps household one is left with the possibility of a strange psychological puzzle, 'that of whole households suffering collective hallucination or conspiring together to tell stories that are bound to get them laughed at'.

Orwell concluded that poltergeist activity was rooted in the human and probably involved 'a rare and interesting form of insanity'.

'It's obvious, isn't it?' says Paige, after she's read the section on the Phelps case in *Poltergeists*. 'It's all so screamingly *Freudian*. The children's father had died only three or four years earlier. So the older children hated mummy finding a replacement and sharing his bed. And if the mother was involved then it might suggest she didn't find the new man in her bed all that congenial.'

'A depraved sexual appetite? The minister, I mean.'

'Something like that. So she and the kids decided to trash the place. After all, Dr Phelps was a true believer in all that paranormal crap. They used his weakness to get their revenge.'

'Or maybe,' – the thought has just occurred to me – 'they just didn't like his house. He didn't want to move – old men never do – so they decided to try and provoke him into moving somewhere less *disturbed*.'

Paige sucks on her forefinger. 'Yeah, that's possible, I guess.'

'But the minister was a tough nut. He stuck it out for eighteen months and wouldn't budge. So they gave up.'

'Something like that.'

'But we agree that it all boils down to sex? That's what Orwell thought. And sex can drive you mad.'

Paige smiles and leans forward and rests her hand on my knee.

Outside I can hear the waves crashing against the pier.

An unending sequence of big rising curling rushes of water that thump against the long line of rusty supports before finally exploding in a big milky boiling surge.

14 Oink! Oink!

THERE ARE PIGS EVERYWHERE around Southwold.

If you look north you can see them on the sloping land behind the cliffs. A vast pig farm. Mostly the stench blows away on the wind but just occasionally it drifts south to mingle with the aroma of hops from the brewery.

To the west, along the banks of the Blyth, there's another large pig farm. Hundreds of porkers, gloriously wallowing in the mud.

In *Animal Farm* pigs are Stalinists. They corrupt the revolution and seize control, becoming no better than the human rulers they displaced.

But the novel had its origins in Orwell's encounter not with pigs but with a horse. In a country lane he saw a small boy leading a large cart horse. It suddenly struck him how things might be if animals had consciousness of their strength against the weakness of those who controlled them.

In his book *1985* Anthony Burgess identified the horse as that enormous type known as a *Suffolk Punch*. This fact existed only in his imagination. Orwell never named the species of horse he saw that day. But I like the idea of a Suffolk connection.

Paige isn't very interested in *Animal Farm*.

Since the collapse of the Soviet Union it has lost its edge. It's now a museum piece. Nothing dates faster than political satire. Stalin is just a name, a pale and distant ghost. The evolution of post-revolutionary Russia in the twentieth century is now just a matter for historians.

'*Animal Farm* is also riddled with sexism,' she snorts, as we wander along a narrow footpath that extends inland along the northern boundary of Buss Creek. The pig farm is very close and we can see the animals, heads down in the mud, foraging.

'The female animals are all stereotypes. They're either stout and motherly like Clover or shallow and vain like Mollie the pretty white mare. Mollie is entranced by the contents of the farmer's wife's dressing-table. Women are all the same, you see – whether human or animal.'

'But maybe some women are like that,' I retort, and her eyes flash angrily.

'Remember the cat!' she says.

I don't.

I've forgotten the cat.

The cat is lazy. The cat finds a warm place to lie down. She doesn't listen to a word that Major says in his great set speech at the beginning of the book. The cat is just another version of Mollie. The cat isn't a producer. The cat just wants a comfortable life.

'Orwell's revolution never challenges the social hierarchy of gender. All the old stereotypes are present in *Animal Farm*. The novel celebrates masculinity. The wise animals are always male. They are also strong and virile and often brave. The female animals are always subordinated to male prerogatives. And they are divided into two groups. The good female animals incarnate maternal values. They are mothers, carers, nurturers. And then there are the bad female animals – vain, shallow, and concerned only with their appearance and their comfort.'

Paige stops and looks at me. Her eyes are still blazing. 'Orwell not only fails to challenge gender domination. His revolution relies on the persistence of patriarchy as an institution!'

And then her gaze shifts past me and beyond my shoulder. 'Oh. My. God.'

I swing round to see what's making her stare like that.

And when I do I break into laughter.

Beyond the humming electrified wire which separates the field of pigs from the path, an enormous boar has mounted an even bigger pig. The animals are immense – almost as big as small cars. The forelegs of the boar are clamped to the pale flanks of the bigger pig, which continues to press its snout into the muddy ground, indifferent to the sexual activity occurring at its rear.

Congress has yet to be achieved. Inch by inch the boar hauls itself further along the back of its object of desire. Its vast haunches sway as it seeks to press itself closer.

It takes rest breaks as it nudges itself closer to its target.

'It's grotesque,' Paige whispers.

I squeeze her hand. 'It's making me feel kinda sexy,' I reply.

She grins. 'You are *sick!*'

'I think we should feel inspired.' I glance up and down the path. You can see for several hundred yards in each direction and there's no one in sight.

'It's too cold,' she says, shaking her head.

'Cold is sensuous,' I say.

And then we are behind the hedge. She peels her knickers and jeans off and crouches on all fours. We both come very quickly.

Beside us a line of porkers regards us curiously.

We put our clothes back on and depart.

In the field the boar is still struggling its way forward, not quite yet there...

Yes, these are happy pigs, living an outdoor existence.

Until the day comes when they get transported to the abattoir and have their throats cut.

A reflection which makes me think of that brilliant Weezer song, 'Pig'.

The reviews of *Animal Farm* were often lukewarm. Isaac Rosenfeld in *Nation* wrote the kind of review that every author can do without. He wanted the book written differently. He wanted the parable *expanded*. How? Why? To incorporate the complexity of history. But parables by their nature flatten out and simplify. You can't write a parable that is also a complex, epic historical novel. But Rosenfeld's review wasn't really about Orwell's use of literary form. Rosenfeld plainly had a soft spot for Stalin and the Soviet Union, which he conflated with what he was pleased to call 'Marxism':

> If Marxism has really failed, the most ironic thing about its failure is that it should be attributed to the piggishness of human nature. It is at this point that a failure of imagination – failure to expand the parable, to incorporate into it something of the complexity of the real event – becomes identical with a failure in politics.

Animal Farm, huffed and puffed the long forgotten Mr Rosenfeld, 'can only be called a backward work'.

That rather more distinguished figure, Edmund Wilson (pal of Nabokov and author of the classic *To the Finland Station*), did what a reviewer should do. First of all he described what the book was about ('a satirical animal fable about the progress – or backsliding – of the Russian Revolution'). Second, he offered a critical evaluation as to how well the author had achieved his design:

> Mr Orwell has worked out his theme with a simplicity, a wit, and a dryness that are closer to La Fontaine and Gay, and has written in a prose so plain and spare, so

admirably proportioned to his purpose, that *Animal Farm* seems very creditable if we compare it with Voltaire and Swift.

Graham Greene liked *Animal Farm*. 'It is a sad fable,' he wrote in the *Evening Standard*, 'and it is an indication of Mr Orwell's fine talent that it is really sad – not a mere echo of human failings at one remove.'

Kingsley Martin in the *New Statesman and Nation* shared the other reviewer's admiration for the fable but he detected a change in Orwell's personality. Where Greene saw melancholy, Martin saw something altogether more corrosive. *Animal Farm* 'suggests to me that he is reaching the exhaustion of idealism and approaching the bathos of cynicism':

> The logic of Mr Orwell's satire is surely the ultimate cynicism of Ben, the donkey. That, if I read Mr Orwell's mind correctly, is where his idealism and disillusion has really landed him. But he has not quite the courage to see that he has lost faith, not in Russia but in mankind.

'Smart guy, Kingsley Martin,' says Paige. 'He saw where Orwell was heading. And *Nineteen Eighty-Four* represents the climax of that disillusion and despair.'

Shrewdly, Graham Greene saw the book's cinematic potential: 'If Mr Walt Disney is looking for a real subject, here it is: it has all the necessary humour, and it has, too, the subdued lyrical quality he can sometimes express so well.'

Enter the Central Intelligence Agency, who beat Walt to it.

The CIA set up a front organisation, Touchstone Inc., to subsidise the filming of the novel.

Touchstone is strangely similar to *Treadstone* – the black ops CIA unit which supplies the plot of all the Jason Bourne movies (which I love – Paige is less enamoured. But then Jason Bourne movies are films for boys).

Was 'Treadstone' an Orwellian pun? Or am I now so sunk in Orwell that I see him everywhere?

That's always the danger with obsessions. You end up with a kind of reverse-paranoia.

A movie contract was signed in October 1951. The producer was Louis de Rochement, who was best mates with FBI director J. Edgar Hoover. The animators chosen for the task were two top grade professionals who ran their own studio in Britain, John Halas and Joy Batchelor – a husband and wife team.

A cartoon *Animal Farm* was in reality a radical proposal. At this point in time there had only been around twenty animated features in the history of cinema, the majority made by Disney. *Animal Farm* was going to be the first serious cartoon movie as well as the first one ever manufactured in Britain for commercial distribution.

The script was where the problems were. Halas and Bachelor wanted to stick to the book. Treadstone – sorry, Touchstone – wanted Significant Alterations. They wanted it spelled out to the audience that Napoleon the pig was Stalin, with a pipe and *black bristles, more or less curved to suggest the Stalin mustache.* It had to be made obvious that Snowball was Trotsky, with whiskers *somewhat suggestive of the Trotsky goatee.*

And Touchstone wanted only one bad farmer. Farmer Jones was inescapable. You couldn't make the movie without him. At the same time one didn't wish to antagonise the powerful American agriculture lobby... Touchstone *scoured the scripts for any nuances that might undermine their political agenda, however unlikely such things were to be noticed by the vast majority of the viewing audience.* Writes Danial J. Leab, Professor of History, who wrote a book on the subject, *Orwell Subverted: The CIA and 'Animal Farm'.*

Touchstone wasn't happy with Snowball-Trotsky. The script made him too sympathetic: 'intelligent, courageous, dynamic'. Like he was in the original novel... The CIA fretted about the implications. An audience might get the impression that if Snowball hadn't been liquidated he might have succeeded in creating a benevolent and successful society. This hypothetical nuance could *not* be permitted.

The instruction went out: Snowball must be shown to be 'an impractical visionary' and a 'fanatic intellectual whose plans if carried through would have led to disaster no less complete than under Napoleon'. There was dissent but the producer, Louis de Rochement, agreed to the changes. With each script-rewrite, Snowball's character grew more unsympathetic. He became more officious and haughty.

And it got worse.

The original script contained the 'apparent inference that Communism is good in itself but that it was betrayed by Stalin & Co'. Worse, there was the suggestion that capitalism was bad (the animals do all the work, the men laze around giving orders). The script failed to bring in 'the large scale defections' by Soviet troops in the Second World War. Some leftists who watched the film as scripted might find their sympathies orientated to the Soviet experiment and build up a resistance to the allegory.

Touchstone also wasn't happy with the idea of animals being thrilled to hear about the revolution at Manor Farm.

They wanted scenes with contented cats and fat calves, which were thriving under a benign capitalism run by kindly, smiling farmers. They wanted a scene in which a sheepdog walking alongside a friendly farmer hears about the revolution and laughs it to scorn.

Touchstone got what it wanted. Those invented scenes, not found in *Animal Farm*, all appear in the movie.

They even wanted a plough horse driven by another jolly farmer. The horse hears about the revolt of the animals and laughs in incredulity.

Touchstone got that too, even though it directly reverses the original idea of the novel, which came to Orwell after he returned to England in 1937:

> On my return from Spain I thought of exposing the Soviet myth in a story that could be easily understood by almost anyone and which could be easily translated into other languages. However, the actual details of the story did not come to me for some time until one day (I was then living in a small village) I saw a little boy, perhaps ten years old, driving a huge cart-horse along a narrow path, whipping it whenever it tried to turn. It struck me that if only such animals became aware of their strength we should have no power over them.

Even de Rochemont was starting to get uneasy about Touchstone's impact. 'The money interests are now asking for complete editorial control,' he complained. But what Touchstone wanted, Touchstone got.

The biggest transformation of Orwell's novel occurred at the end. In *Animal Farm* the book the animals are betrayed and defeated. The ending is as pessimistic as *Nineteen Eighty-Four*'s was to be. The animated version proposed a new climax in which the animals 'get mad, ask for help from the outside, which they get, and which results in their (the Russian people) with the help of the free nations overthrowing their oppressors'. A fantasy re-run of the outcome of the Russian civil war, rewriting history.

Incredibly, in the final scene, there are no men – just pigs. The entire point of Orwell's satire is neutered. His docile and defeated animals are transformed into rebels once again, rising up against pig tyranny. The pigs are driven out. It's a sexy, action-packed upbeat ending.

'A cartoon film with no women,' says Paige, dryly. Unsmiling. Stone cold serious.

'But there weren't any in the book!'

My smile is of the triumphant variety.

'Yes, there were. Farmer Jones had a wife. How interesting that you don't remember her. Typical of the male intellect.'

'Don't generalise,' is the best retort I can manage. I crawl off the battlefield, wounded, and go and pour myself a beer.

I offer Paige one but she shakes her head.

'The mares Clover and Mollie were cut out of the movie too,' she adds.

She's right. I didn't notice that.

Isaac Rosenfeld spotted something about the original book which everyone else who wrote about the novel missed. Napoleon was Stalin and Snowball was Trotsky but 'for simplicity's sake, Vladimir Ilyich [Lenin] is left out of the picture'.

Simplicity?

If so, it was *simplistic*.

Christopher Hitchens on *Animal Farm*: 'As an allegory

the story has one enormous failure: the persons of Lenin and Trotsky are combined into one, or, it might be even truer to say, there is no Lenin-pig at all. Such a stupendous omission cannot have been accidental (especially since it recurs in *Nineteen Eighty-Four*, where there is only Big Brother on the one hand and Emmanuel Goldstein on the other).'

Spot on, Mr Hitchens.

But wait!

Here comes Richard Seymour, writer, journalist, activist, and former member of the Socialist Workers Party. Seymour, author of *Unhitched: The Trial of Christopher Hitchens* (2012). Not to mention a book about Jeremy Corbyn and one with the provocative title, *The Liberal Defence of Murder*.

Unhitched has a section on Orwell and Hitchens.

Seymour accuses Hitchens of white-washing Orwell – the Orwell who, towards the end of his life, produced a list of 135 subversives. A list which was suppressed by the Orwell Archive, which was plainly aware that it reflected badly on St George.

The people on the list were not simply accused of being Communists or Communist sympathisers – they were *potential saboteurs*.

Seymour suggests why Hitchens was so keen to exonerate Orwell from the criticisms of the left. His identification with him was total. So total that it disabled his interpretative skills:

> Orwell was an ego ideal, so flaws could be admitted – but nothing too fundamental. The obverse of this, naturally, was the bitter scolding of critics who went too far.

Hitchens made no reply to Seymour's charges.

He couldn't.

He'd died the previous year.

15   The List

THE LIST.

In the course of writing a book about Orwell a visiting scholar from the U.S.A. was inadvertently given access to the list.

> I remember clearly my dismay when, in May 1983, I sat in the Orwell Archives at University College, London, and held in my hands the list – or, as I called it in my notes at the time, the Notebook of Names – that Orwell kept toward the end of his life, in which he recorded the names and his appraisal of individuals he considered politically unreliable. When the archivist accidentally delivered to me this notebook, on the cover of which was clearly marked 'Closed, except with Mrs. Orwell's permission,' in a box with other materials, I naturally read it quickly and quietly. Uncertain how to deal with this find at the time, I mentioned it briefly in my book on Orwell, but otherwise did not draw attention to it.

But of course by May 1983 Mrs Orwell was not in a position either to grant or to deny permission. She'd been dead three years. The list wasn't being *suppressed*. It was being *ignored*. It lay in the archives, gently ticking. The explosion was still some years away. And when it came it was detonated not by the list itself but by the revelation of what Orwell had *done* with his list.

Daphne Patai, the visiting American scholar quoted above, wrote in her book on Orwell, 'We do not know what purpose this notebook (primarily in Orwell's own handwriting with occasional notations in another hand) was meant to serve.'

In fact she wasn't the first person to come across the list or to mention it in a book. The list first surfaced, sort of, in Bernard Crick's plodding authorised biography, first published in 1980. And he didn't know what use the list had been put to either.

There's a glancing reference to it in Crick's account of Orwell's last year, when the writer lay in bed in the sanatorium at Cranham, high in the Cotswold hills. There, he was visited by his enduring Southwold love, Brenda Salkeld, and also by Paul Potts, an old Independent Labour Party friend. He had a social life and he kept busy. Orwell wrote to the *News Chronicle* on 3 March, protesting about the death sentence imposed on Enrique Marco Nadal, a Spanish republican. And Orwell also wrote to Vernon Richards, asking him to pass on the message that the Freedom Press was welcome to keep Eileen's typewriter. This was connected to the internal politics of the National Council for Civil Liberties and its Freedom Defence Committee, of which the Communist Party had lost control. Crick adds, 'He worried about Communist infiltration elsewhere, however, and kept a notebook of suspects.'

And that's it, apart from a footnote referring to 'A notebook of 1949' in the Orwell Archive with '86 names of Communists or Communist sympathisers'. However, 'Most of the entries are by another unidentified hand.' The archive entry is not given.

Crick had brought the list out into the open. But his casual and glancing allusion to its existence passed unnoticed.

Nothing to see here, move along please.

Crick was unperturbed by the contents of the list.

Daphne Patai wasn't prepared to let Orwell off so lightly.

It provided, she thought, 'a perfect example of the claustrophobic cold war mentality soon to become embodied in Senator Joseph McCarthy, in which individuals are scrutinized to determine their possible Communist connections and political "reliability". Orwell notes religious affiliations and physical ailments, and attaches labels to identify character, sexual preference (when it deviates from the norm), and politics.'

Patai found the list disturbing. It illustrated – *ZAP!* – 'Orwell's descent into a vigilante mentality' and – *POW!* – 'the smug tone of one totally confident in his judgements of people and ready to label them according to narrow criteria'. It was – *WHAM!* – 'an attitude visibly at odds with Orwell's popular reputation as an opponent of all forms of totalitarianism'.

But this ferocious one-woman guerrilla assault on St George resulted, at best, in merely a few tiny ripples in the big shadowy sluggish lake of academia. *The Orwell Mystique* was published by the University of Massachusetts Press in a year crowded with Orwell books (i.e. 1984). It was not published in the United Kingdom. It didn't go into a second edition. The readership for a scholarly feminist deconstruction of Orwell with a games-theory angle was very small.

And so *the list* stayed unread and unstudied, literally in the dark, inside a cardboard box in the air-conditioned archives of UCL.

An entire decade rolled by.

On 10 July 1996, under the 'open government policy', documents in the Foreign Office files were released by the Public Record Office. They related to the work of The Information Research Department, set up in 1948. This innocuous-sounding body was engaged in propaganda against Communism and the Soviet Union. The material made public included a report by Celia Kirwan, who had visited Orwell at the Cranham sanatorium on behalf of the IRD.

Celia Kirwan was the twin sister of the novelist Arthur Koestler's wife, Mamaine. She'd first met Orwell during Christmas 1945 when they'd both stayed with the Koestlers. She was thirty, attractive and single. Orwell's wife Eileen had died earlier that year. He proposed marriage to Celia but she declined. They remained good friends. When she started work with the IRD she regarded Orwell as someone who might be useful to its work. On 30 March 1949 she went to visit the sick man and reported back:

> Yesterday I went to visit George Orwell, who is in a sanatorium in Gloucestershire. I discussed some aspects of our work with him in great confidence, and he was delighted to learn of them, and expressed his wholehearted and enthusiastic approval of our aims.

Orwell was too unwell to write propaganda for the IRD but he suggested the names of three good writers who might be willing to co-operate. A few weeks later, on 2 May, he mailed Celia 'a list with about 35 names'. These he identified as 'crypto-Communists & fellow travellers'. He explained, 'It isn't very sensational and I don't suppose it will tell your friends anything they don't know. At the same time it isn't a bad idea to have the people who are probably unreliable listed.'

A journalist went to look at the newly opened archive and the story broke in *The Daily Telegraph* two days later: **ORWELL IS REVEALED IN ROLE OF STATE INFORMER.**

'That's a headline you can't quarrel with,' says Paige.

And she's right.

Tom Utley:

An icy blast from the Cold War blew through the Left-wing Establishment yesterday when it was revealed that George Orwell, one of the great heroes of twentieth-century Socialism, had secretly co-operated with the Foreign Office in its propaganda battle against Communism.

Utley phoned around to get reactions. Bernard Crick was ready with his usual large, slopping bucket of cold water. It wasn't news, he harrumphed. It was no surprise at all to Bernard. The notebook with the list had been lying in the archive for at least twenty years. Everybody who saw it realised it wasn't important.

What's more, Professor Crick firmly supported his subject's offer to help the IRD. He wasn't denouncing these people as subversives. He was only denouncing them as unsuitable for a counter-intelligence operation.

'I'm afraid there are some on the Left who still think he went too far. God knows, it's a strange mentality.'

There! Bucket empty!

The List.

In fact, there were two lists. The list of names sent to the IRD was taken from a much longer list contained in a quarto notebook with a stiff pale-blue board cover measuring 19.8 x 16.5 centimetres. The notebook contained 135 names. The names were annotated with comments, often derogatory. Some were marked with a red or blue asterisk but it is not known why.

In the final volume of *The Complete Works of George Orwell*, ninety-nine of these names were published, but thirty-six names were withheld on the grounds that if made available the publishers might be sued for libel. The distinction was basically between those listed who were known to be deceased and others who were either alive or untraceable.

Orwell's annotations ranged from the unflattering to the defamatory. John Alderson, a journalist on *The Manchester Guardian*, was 'stupid'. Louis Adamic, author of *Dinner at the White House*, was identified as 'Some kind of agent (prob.)' The M.P. Richard Crossman was 'Too dishonest to be outright F[ellow] T[raveller].' The novelist and reviewer Arthur Calder-Marshall was an 'Insincere person'. Joseph E. Davies, former American Ambassador to the USSR, was 'Very stupid'. Janet Flanner, who wrote for the *New Yorker*, was a 'Dishonest careerist'. The novelist Douglas Goldring was a 'Disappointed careerist' and 'Probably venal' and a 'Shallow person'. The writer and publisher Ralph Ingersoll was the 'Dishonest demagogic type'. Kingsley Martin, editor of the *New Statesman*, was a 'Decayed liberal' and 'Very dishonest'. Etcetera, etcetera...

How Orwell would have loved Twitter!

It was believed that Orwell sent Celia Kirwan a list of thirty-five names, but after her death a new list was found among her papers, showing that the true number was thirty-eight. These were published for the first time in 2006 in *The Lost Orwell*, a supplement to *The Complete Works*. It included eight names previously held back. But other names remained under wraps and even today, seventy years after Orwell's death, *the full list still hasn't been published*

One of the names listed in the infamous blue notebook

was Sean O'Casey, the Irish playwright who lived in England. Orwell wondered if he was a member of the Communist Party and described him as 'Very stupid'.

O'Casey was not a member of the Communist Party. But he did not disguise his admiration for the Soviet Union. The likelihood of the IRD ever employing him for propaganda purposes was zero.

Here, Orwell was simply working off an old grudge. Thirteen years earlier Victor Gollancz had sent Sean O'Casey a proof copy of *A Clergyman's Daughter*, inviting him to provide a recommendation for the dustjacket. It seems that Gollancz drew O'Casey's attention to the experimental section set at night in Trafalgar Square, which had been inspired by Orwell's enthusiasm for *Ulysses*. Gollancz invited O'Casey to agree that it 'was one of the most imaginative pieces of writing they had ever read – equal to Joyce at his best'. O'Casey declined to supply the required puff. He was of the opinion that 'Orwell had as much chance of reaching the stature of Joyce as a tit has of reaching that of an eagle.'

O'Casey's use of 'tit' was, we can safely assume, invoking more meanings than simply the ornithological one.

Someone in the Gollancz office seems to have told Orwell of O'Casey's hostility. Orwell duly absorbed the insult and let it quietly ferment until, a decade later, he had the opportunity to exact his revenge. He was invited to write a review of *Drums under the Windows*, a volume of O'Casey's memoirs, for the *Observer*, where it appeared on 28 October 1945. The review mixed scraps of grudging admiration – 'the subject matter is valuable and interesting' – with a full-scale assault from beginning to end.

Orwell's snarling, angry review began: 'W. B. Yeats said once that a dog does not praise its fleas, but this is somewhat contradicted by the special status enjoyed in this country by Irish nationalist writers.. Orwell went on to lash

masses of pretentious writing

the cloudy manner in which the book is written

an unbearable effect of narcissism

a Joycean style which is hopeless for narrative purposes

bombast

the worst extremes of jingoism and racialism

Frothing with fury, he made a glancing reference to the Easter Rising and 'the summary execution of some twenty or thirty rebels' – Orwell's casual indifference to the exact number is telling. He then perversely asserted that 'Easter 1916' 'is not one of Yeats's better poems', a truly bizarre judgement driven not by aesthetic considerations but by personal prejudice. With staggering hypocrisy he then argued that the problem with the good press that Irish writers received (an assertion for which he supplied no evidence) was that 'literary judgement is perverted by political sympathy, and Mr O'Casey and others like him are able to remain almost immune from criticism. It is time to revise our attitude for there is no real reason why Cromwell's massacres should cause us to mistake a bad or indifferent book for a good one.'

Orwell's own literary judgement was *perverted*, not by politics but by the rancour he still felt for O'Casey's contemptuous response to *A Clergyman's Daughter*.

He raged about O'Casey's 'bombast' and 'jingoism' and quoted as an example the four lines of poetry which the Irish author had used in his representation of Cathleen ni Houlihan. O'Casey replied, pointing out that in his fury Orwell had failed to recognise the fact that the lines he perceived as an instance of Irish fanaticism were actually written by Alfred Lord Tennyson. *The Observer*, run by Orwell's chum The Honourable David Astor, did not print his letter. It was passed on to Orwell. Orwell did not reply.

O'Casey had a right to feel aggrieved. Besides, as the pugnacious street-fighter type, he wasn't going to let Orwell get away with his vicious review. But by the time he retaliated the year was 1954 and Orwell was four years dead. That retaliation came in the sixth volume of his autobiography, *Sunset and Evening Star* (more Tennyson!), which covered the years 1934-1953. O'Casey devoted a chapter to his adversary, mocking 'Rebel Orwell': 'he was a sergeant in the Burma police all right, for the sergeant's shout echoes strongly in a lot of his work; and, particularly, in the persistent egotism that all should think as he thought, or suffer for it'.

Orwell was an assistant commissioner, not a sergeant, but you can see what O'Casey was getting at.

Animal Farm wasn't original, asserted O'Casey:

A similar tale appears the time the English language was beginning to be timidly lisped in a welter of French and Latin. It appears in a poem called Vox Clamantis, written by Gower when he was frightened to death by the rising of the peasants led by Wat Tyler and John Ball. Gower tells of the crowd changed into beasts, asses fierce as lions, who will bear no more burdens, oxen who refuse to draw the plough, dogs who bark at huntsmen; all led by a

Jay, representing Tyler, who harangues them, probing the air with shouts of Down with the honourables, Down with the Law!

As for *Nineteen Eighty-Four*...

Orwell had quite a lot of feeling for himself; so much, that, dying, he wanted the living world to die with him... he prophetically destroyed world and people in Nineteen hundred and eighty-four: Doomsday Book. The decay in himself was in his imagination, transmuted into the life of the whole world. Well, if that isn't self-pity, wrapped sourly up in yearned revenge, then nothing is.

'*Men*,' says Paige, with a snort. 'And you have the nerve to invent the adjective *bitchy* about women.'

'Hey,' I reply. 'Not me personally. Don't generalise.'

Paige reads O'Casey's chapter. 'You missed out the most important bit. That's where he quotes Orwell's friend Arthur Koestler. He said Orwell had "an odd glamour: the farther away he was, the more one liked him". I think that's so true. The man was flawed and at times repellent.'

'Maybe. Nobody's perfect.'

'Oh *please*. Don't be trite.'

'And Koestler was allegedly a serial rapist.'

'You're kidding me.'

'No, I'm not. There's a biography. It's all there. Next to Koestler, Orwell is Mr Nice Guy.'

Silence.

Paige eventually says: 'Do you think O'Casey was the inspiration for O'Brien in *Nineteen Eighty-Four*? I mean, the name is Irish. And O'Brien amounts to what Orwell accused O'Casey of being: a cuckoo in the nest. O'Casey lived in England, a state he explicitly detested. He was an Irish patriot who chose not to live in the Republic. Likewise O'Brien is a fierce critic of Big Brother. But he's actually complicit in the system. A collaborator whose role is to trap traitors like Winston Smith. O'Brien represents smooth-talking betrayal.'

'I hadn't thought of that. It's possible, I suppose. I need to re-read the book and consider it.'

And the waves crash along the shore.

16 Big Bang

WHY DID ORWELL go to Jura?

Barnhill was in a remote part of an island off the Scottish coast which was difficult to get to – especially for people who lived and worked in London.

Sure, he wanted to get away from his friends and acquaintances and hangers-on and write his new novel, *The Last Man in Europe*.

But if you want to cut yourself off from your friends you don't need to go that far. He could just as easily have rented a house in a remote part of Cornwall. Or Kent. Or Yorkshire.

Of course, Orwell had for some years dreamed of escaping to the Hebrides. But after 1945 there was a new urgency.

Orwell's friend Tosco Fyvel thought he had the answer: 'he wanted to put the maximum distance between himself and the atomic threat'.

Hiroshima and Nagasaki: the annihilation of those cities lent new urgency to Orwell's rush north. He also had the responsibility of caring for his adopted son, Richard. Best get the boy away from atomic radiation...

Fyvel and Orwell often used to quarrel about Palestine and Zionism. But from Jura Orwell sent a letter to Fyvel telling him to stop fretting about the Middle East, 'because we might all be blown up in five or ten years'.

If the world is going to end it is important to finish one's novel, is it not? *The Last Man in Europe*. A dystopian title. Later changed to a year. Which brings me to the wisdom of professors.

For example, Alan Kennedy, Professor of English and Chair of the English Department, Dalhousie University. In 1990 he published a work of criticism, with the racy title,

Reading Resistance Value: Deconstructive Practice and the Politics of Literary Critical Encounters.

It included this pearl of wisdom about *Nineteen Eighty-Four*: 'Public interest in the novel has now virtually disappeared, and is unlikely to reappear now that the year of the book has disappeared into history.'

Dream on, Professor!

December, and the morning sun pours in.

Outside, frost coats the stiff green vegetation along the rim of the cliff. The tiles of the houses look like sugar has been scattered across them.

The brilliant sunlight casts long bands of dark slanting shadow. A couple walk past wearing sunglasses.

After breakfast I walk to the harbour, taking a long circular route back into town. I go into Le Roc for a cappuccino and drink it slowly, reading my new Orwell book. It's another connection I've only just discovered. I exchanged emails with a friend who lectures in literature at Southampton and he's told me about *1985*. A novel I didn't know existed. It was published in 1978, before I was born.

The author is Anthony Burgess. Another writer who has fallen out of fashion and is nowadays little read. Apart from his one enduring title, *A Clockwork Orange*. I suppose I shouldn't be surprised to discover that the author of that little dystopian masterpiece should have been inspired in other ways by *Nineteen Eighty-Four*.

I order a paperback copy from AbeBooks and it arrives promptly.

1985 turns out to be a two-part book. Part Two is Burgess's own version of a nightmarish Britain in the future. I don't have time to bother with that. Some other time, maybe. No, it's Part One I'm interested in. This is where

Anthony Burgess interrogates *Nineteen Eighty-Four* and comes up with his own interpretation.

Or as he puts it (using the royal 'we'):

We have the following tasks. To understand the waking origins of Orwell's bad dream – in himself and in the phase of history that helped to make him. To see where he went wrong and where he seems likely to have been right.

Burgess's challenge to himself throws up some interesting and provocative answers. He asserts that *Nineteen Eighty-Four* 'is essentially a comic book'. By which he means it's a satirical version of London in the 1940s. A seedy, run-down city full of bombsites. A city where the memory of V2 rocket attacks was still fresh. An era when Orwell worked in a windowless basement for a vast, faceless bureaucracy (the BBC). The era of state propaganda. In short, *Nineteen Eighty-Four* is not a prophetic vision of the future, merely the present given a slight and savage twist.

And it's packed with autobiography. Orwell describes the gin that Winston Smith drinks as giving off 'a sickly oily smell, as of Chinese rice-spirit'. Burgess comments: 'How could Winston know that? That's the author himself, late of the Burma police, getting in the way.'

The past is important to Orwell. But the problem is, Burgess argues, 'There's a part of Orwell which fears the future. Even when it's Socialist, progressive, just, egalitarian. He wants to oppose the past to it.'

And Orwell can't see working-class people as individuals. In *Animal Farm* he pictures them as 'noble and powerful, like Boxer the horse'. In *Nineteen Eighty-Four* hope lies with the proles, but the idea seems like a fantasy. The working-class mother that Winston watches, admiring her 'mighty loins' is like a cartoon figure from a Soviet propaganda poster. 'At the end of his literary career Orwell dropped all pretence of believing in the working class,' Burgess concludes. '*Nineteen Eighty-Four* is not a prophecy so much as a testimony of despair.'

I think he's right.

I lend Paige *1985* and she returns it next day. (Like me, she skipped the fiction half.)

She's not impressed.

'Just like a man,' she sighs. 'Burgess really doesn't see that Orwell's contempt for women is as strong in *Nineteen Eighty-Four* as in all his earlier books. Just look at Winston's mother, say. A woman with a good heart and limited intelligence. Just like the proles, the natives, the blacks, and women in general.

'At the other extreme is Julia. Because she's sexually active she's regarded as corrupt. Depraved. And that not only excites Winston. It excites Orwell. He's basically reproducing the old Madonna/whore stereotypes. He's in raptures about mothers. Childbearers. Self-sacrificing maternal women. But always dependent on men. Wives. So you see what Orwell is up to? He fetishisizes power without ever noticing male power over women.'

She's wearing her pugnacious face again. Chin tilted up, eyes fiery.

It's like *I'm Orwell.*

In the dock.

The accused.

A perfidious male.

She's not finished.

'You know what I think? I think Winston's beef with the

Inner Party and Big Brother is that they monopolise masculinity. They've made him weak and fearful. Winston Smith is an honorary woman. And *Nineteen Eighty-Four* is an expression of *gender repression*. Orwell is fixated on dominance and submission. But those who submit can never rebel in Orwell's scenario because they lack consciousness. Consciousness is always the preserve of the solitary male. And when the solitary male – Winston Smith – is broken by the big boys, all hope is lost. Orwell's despair is the last gasp of a misogynist.'

'I'm not sure about that,' I retort.

'You wouldn't be.'

'What's that supposed to mean?'

'I mean it's hard for a man to see these things. Orwell was a prick. A prick haunted by the terror of detumescence.'

'Cute.'

'Don't fucking patronise me!' Paige looks angry. Furious. There's a blush under those golden Californian cheeks.

'Sorry.'

There's a long silence.

We are sitting at Suzie's beachfront café. No one there but us. Christmas is looming. Hence the tall slim wooden pyramid which has been erected at the back of the café, by the steep concrete steps leading down to the beach from the Sailors' Reading Room.

I guess I'm a coward. I don't want to quarrel with Paige. She's the expert. But for all that her reading of *Nineteen Eighty-Four* isn't mine. I see the book as the feverish outpourings of a sick man. It's a brilliant poem in prose. And although Orwell was unquestionably a shit towards women it's his prose we judge him by, not his failings as a human being. Ditto T. S. Eliot. He may have had some dodgy views about Jews but *Four Quartets* rises above the prejudices of the poet. And maybe all important writers are slightly deranged and abnormal. Nice well-balanced people don't write poetry and novels that endure. The great artists are all fucked-up in one way or another...

The girl behind the counter must have flipped a switch, because suddenly the wooden pyramid lights up. It's only just gone three but already the light is fading. The sky is eighty-per-cent blue, with a layer of cloud over the horizon. There are lots of roly-poly horizontal cotton wool clouds, and behind them is a single white billowing mass of cauliflower cloud. Plus on the horizon is a stationary tanker and, south of it, a big red vessel churning the waters at speed.

There's a chill in the air.

It's at odds with the blue sky and the white clouds and the calm sea where the only waves are tiny rollers breaking on the strand.

'Can I read your book?'

'Only when it's published.'

'Do I get a freebie?'

'Fuck you, buster.'

'I hope so. Again and again.'

'Ha bloody ha. Buy a copy. Boost my income. Help me towards the dream of a pool in the shape of a kidney.'

'A lung would be better. It would be Orwellian.'

'You know something, Benjamin? You really are *a sick fuck.*'

Playback: 'Orwell's socialism is a battleground, best avoided by those who do not wish to find themselves in a slough of hot-tempered tedium,' said John Sutherland.

A slough is a swamp. It is a mire. Or it can be a backwater, a marshy inlet.

Although I see what our distinguished and racily readable Professor Sutherland is getting at, I think he's chosen the wrong metaphor.

Ladies and gentlemen, *Daily Mail* readers, comrades!

Let me propose in its place a mirror.

Orwell is a mirror in which everyone sees themselves.

I said that.

Peter Sedgwick: 'Cynics are, quite simply, people who have no hope and therefore have no capacity to express any demands for the future and the cynic cannot really be a critic; the radical who is only a radical nihilist or a radical tragedian, is for practical purposes, the most adamant of conservatives.'

'I've fucked up my life,' said Sonia Orwell not long before her death. 'I'm angry because I've fucked up my life.'

I learn from D. J. Taylor that Orwell published almost two million words in the course of a relatively short writing life of twenty years.

'Spread out sheet by sheet,' says Taylor, they would occupy 'an area roughly the size of Norwich city centre.'

I'll bear that in mind if ever visit that city.

'Take him to Room 101.'

'No, not that! For God's sake, anything but that!"

'What's in Room 101?'

'The Orwell biographers.'

He started out as a saint, reputation-wise. Yes, *really*.

Christopher Hollis on the late George Orwell, 1956:

I saw an extremely tall, thin man, looking more than his years, with gentle eyes and deep lines that hinted at suffering on his face. The word 'saint' was used by one of

his friends and critics after his death and – well –
perhaps he had a touch of that quality.

The beatification of St George occurred exactly seven days
after he died. 'George Orwell was the wintry conscience of a
generation,' asserted the obituary in the *New Statesman*.
'He was a kind of saint' whose 'instinctive choice' was that
of 'spiritual and physical discomfort'.
    Not everyone saw it like that.

The indictment.
    *Eric Arthur Blair, alias P. S. Burton, alias George
Orwell, in the Court of History, you are charged with the
following crimes.*
    *That you did seek to rape Jacintha Buddicom on or
about September 1921.*
    *That you were a bellicose opponent of birth control and
insisted on sexual intercourse without the use of any
contraception, indifferent to the impact of an unplanned
pregnancy upon a woman – particularly in an era when
pregnancy outside marriage was regarded as shameful
and deplorable.*
    *That you are an incorrigible philanderer and did make
your first wife Eileen deeply unhappy.*
    *That though posing as straight-talking moralist you did
make regular use of prostitutes throughout your adult life.*
    *That in order to evade income tax you became in 1947
'George Orwell Productions Ltd'*
    *That one of your favourite rhetorical devices as a
polemicist was the blanket generalisation ('all ---- are', 'all
---- know ----').*
    *That you did combine this strategy with a voice-of-the-
people posture, using the word 'everyone' ('everyone*

knows that ----', 'all thinking people/decent people/honest people/sensitive people know that ----').

That you did pose as a voice in the wilderness and the standard bearer of truth against the dishonesty of others with whom you disagreed and therefore that your style was coercive and authoritarian.

That you compiled lists of names of people you disliked for a variety of motives, identifying them in derogatory terms and passing on many of these names to the British intelligence services as subversives.

No! He was a hero.

V. S. Pritchett:

I see a tall emaciated man with a face scored by the marks of physical suffering. There is the ironic grin of pain at the ends of kind lips, and an expression in the fine eyes that had something of the exalted and obstructive farsightedness one sees in the blind; an expression that will suddenly become gentle, lazily kind and gleaming with workmanlike humour. [...]

He was an expert in living on the bare necessities and a keen hand at making them barer.

George Woodcock chimed in with his memories of Orwell. Recalling his wartime visits to Orwell's apartment in Canonbury Square, he also compared the writer to a religious icon:

By the fireplace stood a high-backed wicker armchair, of an austerely angular shape which I have seen nowhere else, and here Orwell himself would always sit, like a Gothic saint in his niche.

The *Observer* also saluted Orwell's embrace of austerity, referring to the postwar years: 'He chose to live on a lonely island in the Hebrides, with his adopted baby son, without even a charwoman to look after him.'

Paige snorts. 'What's a charwoman?' she drawls, and I explain.

'Jesus!' she shrieks. 'A man with a child and no woman to help him. What a total hero!'

'Actually,' I say, 'the *Observer* got that wrong. After his first wife Eileen died Orwell hired a housekeeper named Susan Watson. She was twenty-five and recently separated from her husband. She looked after him and then went with him to Jura. But when sister Avril turned up there was friction. Susan always called her employer "George" but Avril screamed that his real name was *Eric*. Avril basically edged Susan Watson out. She wanted her brother all to herself.'

Susan Watson. It struck her that, although Orwell was freshly bereaved, he didn't show any signs of being upset. 'Maybe I was unobservant,' she told one interviewer, 'but I didn't notice any grief in him whatsoever. Absolutely not.'

The austerity stuff contains a grain of truth but it can be overdone. *Was* overdone.

The house in Wallington which Orwell shared with Eileen was very basic in its facilities. But hanging on the wall, proudly displayed, was the portrait of an ancestor, Lady Mary Blair. The couple dined using the Blair family silver (a wedding present from mother and father in Southwold). Brass candlesticks graced the house. They drank wine with dinner – an extravagant luxury for most of the population in the 1930s.

And in the post-war years George Woodcock fondly remembered Orwell taking him out for an 'excellent' and 'lavish' lunch at a London restaurant. They began with an aperitif, washed down the meal with wine and finished with brandy. The bill was six guineas – a very large amount to pay for lunch for two in the 1940s.

And not everyone found Orwell saintly.

Isaac Deutscher, who later wrote an acclaimed multi-volume biography of Trotsky, shared a room with Orwell when they were both working as journalists in Germany in 1945. Deutscher had written commentaries on Russia for *The Economist, The Observer* and *Tribune,* and Orwell had read and liked them. Orwell seemed to agree with his analysis. But then their differences emerged.

I remember that I was taken aback by the stubbornness with which Orwell dwelt on 'conspiracies,' and that his political reasoning struck me as a Freudian sublimation of persecution mania. [...] What struck me in Orwell was his lack of historical sense and of psychological insight into political life coupled with an acute, though narrow, penetration into some aspects of politics and with an incorruptible firmness of conviction.

A few weeks before Orwell died, Deutscher was in New York. In among the newspapers and magazines of a newsagent's store he saw copies of *Nineteen Eighty-Four.*

'Have you read this book?' said the news vendor. 'You must read it, sir! Then you will know why we must drop the atom bomb on the Bolshies!'

A cute anecdote. But perhaps a little too neat, a little too self-rewarding.

17 Various Endings

THERE'S A MAN ON A LADDER in the marketplace, stringing a line of coloured bulbs to a lighting column. In the supermarket next to Church Street there's a shelf filled with small plastic trees and chocolate coins wrapped in gold foil. Christmas is coming, full of possibility and existentialist choices. And Paige is in a café somewhere, writing her last chapter.

That's what she tells me.

Later I find out it's true.

I'm not in the mood for Orwell this morning. I feel I've reached a dead end with Eleanor and Dennis and Eric and those tangled years, 1932-1934.

As Donald Rumsfeld might have said, I now know all I'll never know.

I've gone as far as I can in finding stuff out. Someone else will have to write the conclusion.

I walk to the harbour and watch a trawler coming back with its catch, trailing a cloud of squealing agitated gulls.

I watch a woman of about my own age lining up a shot with her telephoto lens. The lens is about as long as my arm. She takes a dozen shots of the trawler then, when it's gone by, she walks on.

Then she pauses, raises her lens again.

She seems to be focused on a cormorant which is perched on a wooden pole the far side of the river.

Beyond it, looming above a belt of trees, is the tower of Walberswick church. She shoots, then puts a cap over the lens and slings the camera over her shoulder.

She sees me watching and gives me a friendly smile. A blue-eyed blonde, with all the self-assurance of the species.

She knows the default response of the male is worship.

She passes me and goes into the harbour café. She's slim, wearing tight blue jeans and a quasi-military green parka.

Another time, maybe. Not today. Not now.

I walk as far as The Harbour Inn. It's a quiet day, not many cars parked outside. The outdoor wooden tables are all unoccupied.

I take the path that runs across the field at the back of the pub. I cross the Common and enter the copse which shields the road at the southern edge of town. I emerge from it and pass the first terrace of houses, then take a turn to the right. I take the path that leads up Gun Hill and then dips down to the tea room.

Where the path forks I turn left, towards the Casino and the cannons. The path curves back into town and that's where I meet them.

Coming up Gun Hill towards me.

At first I don't recognise her. She's cut her hair – radically. It's practically as short as Paige's. I don't recognise him either. But then I've only ever seen him in photographs.

He's much bigger than I imagined. A six-footer, but gone to seed. Fleshy, with a discernible paunch. A loud – a *very* loud – voice. A navy blue Burberry with epaulettes. The coat flaps around his kneecaps. On a thinner man it would look good.

His shoes are brown brogues with perforated insteps. Essence of rural elite.

'And I said to Gerald, I said Gerald – '

It's a deep, plummy voice. The kind of voice used to giving commands. The kind of voice whose volume control is always set to maximum.

'Gerald, I said – '

There are less than a yard away now. I've moved to one side as they evidently have no intention of stepping out of my line of advance. They cruise on at full throttle. Maybe it's a habit they've picked up steering speedboats.

I recognise Ronnie in the same instant she recognises me. She stops, I stop. Jonny walks past me, then abruptly freezes.

'*Shit!*' she hisses.

'Very good to see you again,' I say, managing to speak in a very calm voice. Maybe I'm just numb with shock.

She regains her composure in seconds. 'Darling!' she shrieks, addressing Jonny, not me. 'This is an old friend of mine.'

Jonny turns back, glaring at me. He reminds me of a fish, pressing its face against the thick wall of an aquarium. Blubbery lips and swollen eyes, like a bloated goldfish with an IQ of minus ten.

'Yah,' he says. At least I *think* that's what he says. But might have been 'baa', like a sheep.

'Ben is a chum of Annette's,' she says, and in that instant I know she's never told her oaf of a husband about those years when we were an item. In fact, Christ knows *what* she's told him. Maybe he's so egocentric he thinks she was a nun until she crossed his path.

'How is Annette?' she asks, coolly.

That's a fucking joke for a start. Annette froze me out, along with everyone else in the set. But this is not the time for recriminations, I tell myself. I'm through with all that.

'I guess she's fine. Just fine,' I say.

I tell myself I mustn't be bitter. Ronnie and I had some good times together. I won't fuck it up for her. I owe her that. I can see the dread in her eyes. The terror that I might spill the jolly old beans and blurt out the truth about our history together.

'And you?'

'I'm fine too.'

'Super.'

'And you?'

'Super also.'

'That's super.'

The goldfish continues to gawp. The sophisticated dialogue between his wife and me is plainly beyond his understanding.

But I'm not going to let her get off so easily.

'Bit surprised to see you here, to be honest. Thought you couldn't stand Suffolk.'

'Goodness, no!' she squeals. 'Can't think where you got *that* idea from.' But there's terror in her eyes: she hasn't forgotten. Her eyes flicker wildly, with a mute appeal to me to say nothing. Nothing that could incriminate her. 'I simply adore Suffolk,' she brays. 'So does Jonny, don't you darling?'

She never used to bray. These days she's obviously spending all her time with donkeys.

'*Rather*, old fruit.'

"Old fruit"! He calls her *old fruit*! It's a struggle not to bellow with laughter. As for her hypocrisy, it's breathtaking.

A quick, strategic change of subject: 'Jonny's just bought that house over there.'

She points towards an enormous detached property with a fabulous view over the sea. It looks like it has about twenty-six bedrooms.

Jonny's eyes light up. Now we are talking his kind of talk! 'Damned sensible investment, property,' he confides. 'Always goes up. Never goes down.'

'You said it,' I say.

But already the goldfish's attention span is broken. The goldfish looks meaningfully at his Rolex. I was thinking of mentioning Vancouver Cottage and saying how we'd be neighbours. But I decide against it. If Ronnie and her hub-tub are seriously thinking of spending time in Southwold, then maybe it's time for me to move on. Recently I've been missing London a lot. The plays, the movies, the exhibitions. Plus I miss my friends.

'Better be getting along, old fruit,' he commands.

'Absolutely,' replies Ronnie, who seems effortlessly to have slipped into the role of a Stepford wife.

'You must come for dinner,' Jonny says.

'Absolutely,' I reply.

But we both know that there will never be an invitation. Jonny is that type. If there's nothing in it for him he won't bother. Once they are back in mansion number nine he'll interrogate her about me and she'll fob him off with some whipped-up froth and he'll suss that I'm a nobody and not worth cultivating.

That's how it goes. And everybody knows.

'Well, cheerio!' Ronnie says, her eyes bright with alarm and anxiety. She's still terrified I'll advert to Ancient History.

'Ciao!' I say, with equal jauntiness.

'Cheery-bye,' says the goldfish, suddenly turning into an octopus as it wraps a fat throbbing tentacle around the woman I once loved.

I look at my watch, which isn't a Rolex. Then I walk on to the pier, where Paige is waiting to tell me something.

Sonia Orwell.

She is conventionally regarded as the model for Julia in *Nineteen Eighty-Four*. Julia is identified as 'the girl from the Fiction Department' and Sonia Orwell worked in publishing as an editor.

I'm amazed to discover that more people wrote novels featuring her as a character than about Orwell himself.

That *louche* Soho drifter Julian Maclaren-Ross was besotted with her. He wrote two books about his infatuation: *Until the Day She Dies* is the tale of a woman pursued by a stalker. It began life as a screenplay, then a radio play and finally a novel. He recycled his obsession with *My Name is Love*. Both novels are long out of print. The first one, 'a tale of terror', can be snapped up for £25. The second one, second hand, will set you back over £1,000. But though Maclaren-Ross was besotted, Sonia was utterly indifferent. Maclaren-Ross's infatuation was strictly a one-way street. It was all in his mind. Sonia was generous with her sexual favours, but Maclaren-Ross was altogether too minor a writer to attract her attention. She was, as one acquaintance brutally put it, a star-fucker. Maclaren-Ross was essentially a nobody. He'd outlived his era, which was the nineteen-forties. By the sixties he was a beached minnow. A sad drunkard hiding behind sunglasses, desperately trying to appear cool and edgy. Hanging out in bars in Soho and Fitzrovia, chatting up the talent, cadging loans, begging for work from chums at the BBC or at *Punch* magazine.

In the earliest stages of his infatuation Maclaren-Ross fantasised that Sonia would find him irresistible. He would reel her in very slowly, then give her the rogering of her life. He wrote to a friend saying that 'The toughest and wisest blokes in London are speculating about the outcome. The betting's on me so far – though this is the most formidable girl I've ever met.'

Pathetic. The self-mythologising just seems wearisome. And Sonia had zero interest in this burned-out, needy pisshead of very limited talents.

She avoided him.

The *grand passion* which Maclaren-Ross fantasized about never happened.

On Wednesday January 25, 1950, a privately chartered twin-engine de Havilland Dove took off from Croydon Airport, en route to the Aéroport de Lausanne-Blécherette in Switzerland. The passengers consisted of Orwell, his wife Sonia, the young painter Lucien Freud and a nurse. There was also a small crate containing a six months' supply of Orwell's favourite Ceylon tea.

The descent to the runway is hair-raising, Sonia later wrote to a friend. *You think you are going to crash into the side of a mountain. Dark pine forests seem to rush at you and then, at the very last moment, the landing strip appears, with its twinkling vanilla lights.*

The party disembarked quickly and a plush private ambulance drove them up winding precipitous roads to The Palace Sanatorium at Montana, high up in the snowy mountains. Here the altitude is 5,000 feet and the pure cold air cuts like a knife.

The little town of Montana-Vermala is located on a small plateau, with spectacular views of peaks and ridges. It's the TB capital of Switzerland, with a whole cluster of sanatoria. Orwell was pleased when Sonia told him that the poet James Elroy Secker had stayed there in the summer of 1913. He was even more excited when he learned that Katherine Mansfield had been a patient at Montana.

The sky was amazing, Orwell remembered. Everything shone, as if charged with electricity. Everything seemed cut out of fresh matter: fresh snow, dense black fir forests, shining silvery streams. The clouds were scooped from cream and rested on a gleaming blue plate. Orwell filled page after page of his notebook with admiring descriptions of the mountain scenery.

Here, in the pure, clean Alpine air Orwell's lungs and body recovered. He inhaled air that was like a rare, expensive perfume. Its fragrance was delicate and muted and cool. It was as if the blossom of orchids had been distilled and diluted with water from a stream trickling out of the dazzling ultramarine tongue of a glacier. There was a hint of conifers. The air, Orwell remembered, was sharp as a surgeon's knife. You could feel it go deep inside your warm body. Sometimes it seemed as sharp as pepper.

He even took up fishing again. How Sonia shrieked with delight when he showed her the big glistening trout he'd caught! Lucien, too, was smitten by the countryside and the magnificent views – as well as by the charms of a local inn-keeper's big-breasted daughter, whom he persuaded to pose nude for a series of sensuous oil paintings which are now recognised for their anticipation of his mature style.

In Switzerland a re-energised Orwell put on weight. A rosy flush appeared on his cheeks. He was able at last to return to his writing table. In just twelve months he finished his new novel about Burma. The critics compared it to *Coming Up For Air*. *A Smoking-room Story* was a Conrad-inflected tale about Curly Johnson, a handsome young English plantation worker returning from Rangoon to Southampton on a P&O liner. The book is a satire about a Ship of Fools. Its portrait of the colonial passengers, including a group of American oil men, is intercut with flashbacks to Johnson's life of drunken squalor in a remote part of Burma.

A Smoking-room Story received mostly rave reviews for its caustic humour, its marvellous evocation of a sultry exotic landscape, and for its melancholy sense of impending annihilation. But not everyone liked the book. The *Daily Mail* found it 'disgusting', 'highly offensive' and 'vicious' for its portrait of a Christian missionary who turns out to be a paedophile, and for the shocking scene in which Johnson and a friend play dice to decide which of them will have sex with a woman and which with her twelve-year-old daughter.

It was only many years later that the book was understood as a metaphor for Orwell's acute foreboding of atomic warfare and the extinction of European society.

The influence of *Heart of Darkness* was noted and the novella was quickly followed by Orwell's critical appreciation of the works of Joseph Conrad. This, too, received high praise from reviewers.

Orwell returned to England, where he and Sonia lived in a handsome five-bedroom cottage on an estate in Buckinghamshire. Roses grew around the porch and at the back was what became known as 'George's menagerie'. It included an aviary, a paddock full of goats, a field of sheep and a dozen squawking, rainbow-winged peacocks.

Their adopted son Richard, away at boarding school much of the year, came home during the holidays. Sonia finished her novel, *The Other Woman*, a thinly disguised account of her affair with the French philosopher Maurice Merleau-Ponty. Writing in the *Sunday Times*, Edna O'Brien called it 'a brilliant diagnosis of the condition of modern woman'. The *Observer* described it as 'better than Simone de Beauvoir'.

The Orwells became Britain's most fêted literary couple. Orwell astonished his admirers by writing *The Eight Bells* – a dazzling detective novel about a series of murders in a sleepy Suffolk seaside town. The critics compared him to Agatha Christie and Margery Allingham at their finest. But he did not neglect his political writings, and wrote a furious attack on the government's involvement in the Suez adventure, as well as a fierce polemic against the Soviet Union for its 1967 invasion of Czechoslovakia. However, his claim that 'this latest spasm of the Stalinist terror, which I have fought against my whole life, might never have happened had the West had the good sense to rearm West Germany' provoked a furious reaction among the left intelligentsia.

His younger admirers were dismayed by his bitter criticisms of popular music and his repeated attacks on The Beatles and The Rolling Stones. Orwell railed against the softness of modern youth and was increasingly seen as a grumpy old man out of tune with the spirit of the sixties. His weekly *Daily Telegraph* column became increasingly querulous and controversial.

Orwell's enthusiastic support for the American war in Vietnam came as a shock. His 1969 essay, 'The Communist Threat', notoriously asserted:

The failure of the 'New Left' (why 'new'?) to connect its critique of American intervention with any responsible plan for an alternative policy is a shocking abdication of responsibility. To orate fluently about American atrocities while passing over those of the Vietcong is a characteristic blindness. To advocate withdrawal without tackling such political human realities as the fate of several million refugees from the North is the familiar and besetting sin of simplification in the face of realities which are messy and irrational.

His support for Margaret Thatcher over the Falklands and then his enthusiastic backing of the Gulf War of 1990, together with his furious critique of the anti-war movement, lost him the support of most of his remaining admirers on the left. His provocative essay in praise of the royal family and his subsequent unexpected acceptance of a knighthood were seen as a further sign of his shift from rebel to establishment man.

Following his sudden death from cardiac arrest in 1992, Orwell was given a state funeral and was buried in Westminster Abbey, with the Prime Minister, the Prince of Wales and Lady Orwell leading the nation in mourning...

But no, it was never going to be like that. He would never have written in the style of his neo-conservative fans, who enlisted him as a posthumous member of their army.

Rewind the clock.

It's now the weekend before the charter flight is due to take off for Lausanne airport and the sanatorium.

This flight will be cancelled.

'Katherine Mansfield,' says Paige. 'Yes, he liked her work. But he also used her as a hammer to attack other women writers.'

She cites Orwell's 1935 review of the novel *The Proceedings of the Society* by Katharine M. Williams. 'It is typically a woman's book (it owes a little to Katherine Mansfield, perhaps),' wrote Orwell, 'in its mixture of sentimentality and disillusionment.'

And the future author of *Nineteen Eighty-Four* complained that 'Miss Williams has clearly a bias in favour of the depressing.'

It's almost The End.

I go and stand by the front door of Montague House for

one last time.

I stare up at the pale stone tablet.

The words are fading fast, washed away by lashing rain. Soft stone is crumbling like salt. There's not much left of Blair. If I didn't know what I know I wouldn't even be able to decipher it. The B and the L are almost vanished.

AIR. That's what it says.

Beautifully apt, really. After all, he wrote *Coming Up For Air*. And he always had breathing difficulties.

By the end of 1949 he was emaciated, with a waxy complexion. *He had so little fat on him that the hospital staff had difficulty finding places on his body where they could give him injections.*

'I've made all this money,' Orwell remarked to one old acquaintance who dropped by to see him. 'And now I'm going to die.'

To another he said, 'I look like a skeleton.'

On January 21, 1950, just after midnight, his body gave up the fight of a lifetime.

A blood vessel in his lung burst. He suffered a massive haemorrhage. The blood kept pouring. *The door to his room had glass panels and a night-light was on, but he wasn't able to ring for a nurse and no one heard his strangled cry for help.*

By the time someone came to check on the patient he was dead.

I always think the best cinematic representation of death, ever, is found at the end of an old Richard Gere movie.

Intersection is by no means one of his best films, although neither is it quite the turkey that some would claim. Richard Gere features as a successful architect torn between two women – his wife and his mistress. He has a car crash, relives his life in flashbacks, and at the end he dies. He's not a particularly sympathetic character, the dialogue is often clunky, and the movie is a remake of a much better French film, *Les Choses de la Vie*. But the cinematography is superb and Gere is, to my mind, an accomplished actor. I don't think I've ever seen a Richard Gere movie that I haven't enjoyed.

At the end of *Intersection*, as he's dying, the Gere character imagines himself on the surface of a dark lake. The two women are in a yacht nearby. He waves at them and shouts for help. But they can't see him or hear him. Slowly they sail away and finally he slips below the surface and vanishes. The End.

I find it a chilling and poignant scene which beautifully captures the loneliness and isolation and finality of death.

In his essay, 'How the Poor Die', Orwell wrote that everyone wanted to die at home, with loved ones at the bedside.

But he died in a hospital room the size of a prison cell, alone.

After Orwell's death it was discovered that in one of his notebooks he had written a passage entitled 'Death Dreams'.

For two years he'd been having vivid dreams. Some were of the sea or the shoreline or ships. Some were of streets or huge magnificent buildings. He entered and lost his way but felt not fear or perplexity but rather a strange, intense happiness. He lost consciousness and woke in bright sunlight.

Death dreams, that's what they were. Orwell saw it all too clearly. They pressed themselves upon him repeatedly at those moments when he despaired of ever recovering but he didn't understand the shape they took. *I am not afraid of death*, he wrote. *Afraid of pain*, yes. *Afraid of the moment of dying*, yes. But not of *extinction*.

His young wife Sonia couldn't hear the cries of a dying man. She was in a nightclub at the time, with her old lover Lucian Freud and his current squeeze, Anne Dunn. They were, in Dunn's words, *winding down with a drink*. Or – *down the hatch!* – perhaps more than one...

It would later be claimed that Sonia had been at the hospital all day until 9pm on 20 January and had been advised to go home and get some rest. Later, when she rang the hospital to check on her husband's progress, she received the terrible news that he'd died.

This was tosh. She wasn't there at all on Orwell's final day. In fact, she hadn't visited him for several days. Nor was there any reason for her to phone the hospital in the middle of the night. The reality is that it was the hospital which tried to contact Sonia to tell her that her husband had died, but there was no reply from her telephone. It rang and rang in her apartment on Percy Street but there was no one there to answer it. Sonia was in the night club, knocking back the booze.

The poet Stephen Spender remembered being with Orwell at the hospital, having a conversation about D. H. Lawrence's death from tuberculosis. Sonia came in and told them to stop talking about it and choose a more cheerful topic. *Then she explained that she had to go to a cocktail party, and would not be back that evening. Orwell protested faintly, but she put him off, in her bustling way.*

You can take your pick.

Which Sonia suits you best? Sonia the flaky drunk, promiscuous and ruthlessly self-centred, a cynical gold-digging star-fucking money-grabber who only married the suddenly affluent Orwell for the sparkling cascade of his royalties? Sonia whose indifference to Orwell's legacy included the destruction of every single letter he'd written to her? *Sonia: the last and most lethal Orwell girl.*

Or would you prefer Sonia the frail, vulnerable woman who always did her best for poor, dear George? Marrying him was a kindness. After his death she did her best to carry out his last wishes. She set up the Orwell archive at University College London. Without Sonia's input, it is argued, the world of Orwell scholarship would be an impoverished place.

You choose.

It was some time after all this was over that I finally understood the end of *Nineteen Eighty-Four*. The clue was always there, lodged in that final paragraph.

Forty years it had taken him to understand what kind of smile was hidden beneath the dark moustache.

That was Orwell speaking about himself. *He* was Big Brother. He was the author; God with a moustache. Omniscient. The one who was always remote, detached, observant. He liked concealment. He hid behind a pseudonym, just like someone on social media or the Thought Police watching and listening to the naked couple on the bed in the room above Mr Charrington's junk shop.

Orwell maintained surveillance. It was like that from the very beginning. He went to Paris and watched. He went into doss houses and observed. He kept notes. The voyeur. The anthropologist. Then he went back to Southwold and wrote it all up. He was O'Brien, jumping from the hideous, seedy world of Victory Mansions into private luxury.

What was he doing all those years ago in Walberswick, in the ruined church? He was watching. He was maintaining surveillance of the road, like a good cop.

Eyeing the girls, probably.

We are on Southwold Pier, a table by the salt-misted window.

Through the glaze I can see big waves roll in and explode noiselessly on the black rocks below. The north beach is as empty as the restaurant.

We are drinking our coffees in silence. The sky is overcast, full of low dark thunderous-looking cloud, with a solitary distant streak of blue. It feels like one season is over and a new one is about to begin. Finally Paige says: 'I'm leaving.'

She stares out at the surf. 'I'm going back to L.A.'

We are always at this table. The waves are always coming in. This conversation is on a loop.

I always knew she'd go back. But I didn't see it as an ending.

'Want me to come with you?'

'I don't think that would be a good idea. Let's say goodbye now, here. I don't want you coming to the airport. Let this end where it began. Sweetly.'

There's a thudding. It takes me a while to realise it's not the rough sea shaking the pier but my heart pumping. My head is a space filled with engine noise. It spreads through my body. It's shaking my chest. My throat feels suddenly dry. I drain my muddy coffee.

'Why should it end now?'

She glances down into the creamy swirl in her cup, then raises her little chin and looks me brazenly in the eyes. 'Because I have a husband.'

A husband!

The word is like a bullet on the Aragon front.

It passes through me and I feel a tremendous shock. It

197

bores through me, twisting my heart. My nerves are screaming.

Catch me, someone. I'm falling.

She grins cheekily. Buoyant in the face of the approaching hurricane. 'Did I forget to tell you?'

I feel stricken; shrivelled to nothing.

I somehow manage to speak. 'When you said you hadn't had sex for over a year...' My voice sounds gravelly and low.

'Yeah, I know. That bit was true. But only because I don't usually cheat on him and we'd normally have met up but then he had to go to Alaska.'

'Alaska?'

'Hell, the details don't matter. He's a mining engineer. But let's not go there. Biography, I mean.'

'That's funny,' I say. 'Bearing in mind us and Eric Arthur Blair.'

She smiles again. 'You know what I mean.'

I did. Every life has its dark corners and its crossroads. Now we were like Orwell and Eleanor Jaques. A couple of people doing the best we could out of the mess called life.

'You're like Eleanor,' I say. 'You've made your mind up. Two men, one choice.'

'That's about the shape of it, buster,' she concedes.

'Off to your Singapore of the heart.' I do a quick calculation. 'Twenty-eight years with another man.' That's how long Eleanor Jaques spent with her other love.

The humour is suddenly gone. Now Paige looks distraught. 'Yeah, baby. Something like that. But a place a whole lot colder than Singapore.'

Get a grip, I tell myself. I feel like bursting into tears. But that would be weak. Tough guys don't cry, as Norman Mailer might have said.

She turns to glance at a herring gull which is in the

process of landing on the railings beyond the windowpane. The bird seems enormous. It stares in at us with black dispassionate eyes. Its beak is bright, egg-yolk yellow. Hooked; predatory. Then it languidly unfolds its wings and rises up and goes winging away over the parallel lines of ocean-battered rock.

She turns back to look at me. 'So what I'm going to do,' she explains, 'is lean over and kiss you. Then I'm going to get up and walk away. My eyes will brim with tears and maybe they'll trickle down my cheeks, but I won't look back. I love you, you bastard, but it's always got to stay here, in this town, for all kinds of reasons.'

She snaps her teeth together, hard. Her eyes are brimming already but I don't say anything. I'm too busy fighting back my own. 'Then when I've gone I want you to stay here and order another coffee. Give me half an hour. I'll be gone from this town by then. And we'll never communicate or meet again. Not even when we are one-hundred years old. No emails, texts or voicemail messages. Not even a fucking Christmas card. Understood?'

I shrug. I nod. I feel a great rage but I crush it. I feel a great love but I seal it up in a vault of silence. For a long, aching phase of time – it can only have been at most a minute – I seem paralysed and deprived of the power of speech. My tongue brushes against my palate, struggling to articulate the opening syllables of a word, and then another word, and then a chain of them that adds up to a sentence.

I manage a bleak smile. 'We'll always have Orwell,' I say, finally.

'You bet, mister.'

Then she leans over and kisses me.

THE END, THE END, THE END

Acknowledgements

George Orwell's connections with Southwold have conventionally been disregarded or marginalised in biographies of the writer. Two exceptions are D. J. Taylor's *Orwell: The Life* (2003) and Ronald Binns's *Orwell in Southwold: His Life and Writings in a Suffolk town* (2018). Anyone interested in seeking out more information about George Orwell and Southwold is advised to start with these two books, which supply helpful biographical material I have drawn on in this novel.

I am also grateful to Gillian Flynn and Paula Hawkins, who with their novels *Gone Girl* (2014) and *The Girl on the Train* (2016) made it acceptable to define adult women as girls. These authors, I point out, are women, which I am not. In its title this novel obviously draws, with a certain discomfort but with one sharp eye on sales, on these monstrously successful examples of commercial prose.

The crumbling stone memorial to Orwell on the wall of Montague House, Southwold, described in the second chapter of this book, was replaced in 2018 by a new, differently worded plaque sponsored by the Orwell Society. The events described in this novel therefore took place no later than 2017.

www.ingramcontent.com/pod-product-compliance
Lightning Source LLC
Chambersburg PA
CBHW031337170626
46807CB00002B/736